THE BESTING OF
HUMPHREY MERCER

THE BESTING OF HUMPHREY MERCER

by

NORMAN ALLEN

*For Nici
with best wishes
Norman Allen
17.07.06*

The Besting of Humphrey Mercer © Norman Allen 2006.

Author has asserted his rights under the Copyright Designs and Patents Act 1988 to be identified as the author of this work.

All rights reserved. No part of this work may be reproduced or stored on an information retrieval system (other than for purposes of review) without the prior permission of the copyright holder.

Published in Great Britain by Twenty First Century Publishers Ltd.

A catalogue record of this book is available from the British Library.

ISBN: 1-904433-54-5.

This is a work of fiction. Names, characters and incidents are the product of the author's imagination or are used fictitiously, and any resemblance to actual persons, living or dead, is entirely coincidental.

This book is sold subject to no resale, hiring out, loan or other manner of circulation in form other than this book without the publisher's written consent.

To order further copies of this work or other books published by Twenty First Century Publishers visit our website:
www.twentyfirstcenturypublishers.com

Illustrations by Norman Allen

For Laurent Bachet, Chris Burton, Tully Crook, Lee Story, Peter Tish, and above all to my darling wife Katherine for her unswerving encouragement.

Chapter 1   The Beginning of the End

Humphrey Mercer's face looked like a death mask: chalky, tired, and cast with a grim frown. His hair was slicked down as always, but he stooped a little rather than standing erect in his usual ramrod, straight-backed fashion. Humphrey Mercer looked as one who'd recently been resuscitated from death as he crept along the corridors of Dynamic House on this gloomy Monday morning, to see who was in. Angela certainly wasn't, if indeed she ever would be, and Digby Hope was taking a break for a few days, to think things over.

Despite it being a good 10 minutes before people normally started arriving at the office, he thought he heard the distant sound of laughter and paused. It seemed to be coming from the floor above, but he couldn't believe that anyone in the creative department would be in yet, especially on a Monday. He shook his head, suspecting the laughter might be within his ringing skull. His tinnitus was louder than usual, and he wondered if he should seek medical advice. In fact his health in general had taken quite a battering over the past several months. He squeezed his forehead hard, wishing the ghastly events of last Friday had been a dream, but he knew all too painfully that they weren't.

The faint peals of mirth rose again and he was sure the sound was imagined. He was certainly not as alert as he was accustomed to feeling and shook his head again. Stephanie Hargreave his P.A. had gone to make coffee, so he turned towards his office looking forward to a soothing warm drink. As he moved laughter filtered down from above him again, but louder this time, and Humphrey Mercer realised that the sounds were not imagined, so he gently mounted the stairs, eschewing the antiquated lift and its uncertain reliability. The laughter stopped, and he stopped.

After a brief quiet moment, a voice broke the silence.

'Pin it to the notice board?' a woman shrieked. 'You can't do that, ee'll go ballistic,' and Susanne Verdier's pretty French laugh rang even louder as the small group in Angus Taylor's office crowded around his desk. Dean Dalton dropped his head sideways and clawed back lank tresses of mousey-brown hair from his crooked face. He stared at the sheet of A4 paper on Angus's desk. Not overburdened with articulacy,

Dean gazed for a while with a look of bovine-eyed wonderment before passing his well considered art director's opinion.

'Isstoo complimentary, innit,' he chuckled. 'I mean, shouldn't it be a bit more insultin'?'

And more obscenely disparaging contributions to the sheet of text were volunteered by the others. Susanne was facing the open door and saw him first. Her sonorous Parisian giggling transmuted to an instant fit of contrived coughing to warn everyone that 'He' was present. The Savile-Row-suited frame of Humphrey Mercer stood predatorily in the doorway.

'I would take something for that cough, if I were you, Miss Vérdier,' Humphrey Mercer's thin, flat voice sarcastically suggested, and at once the room was silent. The Monday morning atmosphere became as cold and depressing as a mortuary. 'May I share in the cause of this merriment, or are we holding a wake?' His stretched mouth curved into an unconvincing smile, more resembling a painful grimace. Angus attempted, surreptitiously, to slide the cause of so much ribaldry under some papers on his desk, but at the speed of a chameleon's tongue Humphrey Mercer's short fingers snatched up the sheet of paper. 'Some of us have got work to do!' he bellowed, saliva splashing from his thin mouth, 'but clearly you lot haven't and after last Friday's fiasco none of you are likely to have in the future!'

He was referring to the recent calamitous new business pitch his advertising agency had made - and he had masterminded - to a Swedish paint manufacturer, the comedy of errors Angus's copywriting was so savagely satirising.

Susanne gave her boss a look of undiluted loathing and confidently strode from the room. She had already tendered her resignation anyway and cared not a jot for this buffoon's threats. The rest of the group quickly followed leaving the office's two official occupants at the mercy of their employer. Humphrey Mercer frowned as he carefully read the poster which was set out in a variety of different typefaces.

The Besting of Humphrey Mercer

**COME TO MAD MERCER'S
ADVERTISING CIRCUS!**
YOU WON'T GIVE US YOUR BUSINESS
*BUT YOU'LL DIE LAUGHING
AT THE WAY WE TRY TO GET IT!*
Hear the world's un-funniest jokes from
the biggest joker of all time
HUMPHREY 'HAVE MERCY UPON US' MERCER!
*You'll cry for mercy when he tells another.
You'll die when you witness the savage throttling
of our marketing director by the mad Pieman!*
THRILL AT THE SIGHT OF THE INCREDIBLE
EXPLODING CARDBOARD PAINT TIN!
A tour de force of farce and ineptitude
Starring: Murky Mercer and his coke snorting pig.

Humphrey Mercer slowly folded the A4 sheet, stuffed it into his pocket and with a face etched with revenge, swivelled on his military heel and left the room without further comment.

Angus looked sick as Dean exhaled a soft whistle before delivering his enlightening opinion. 'I don't think ol' Murky found that very funny.'

Angus slowly shook his head and spat a reply. 'Well, what does the stupid prat expect? The pitch *was* a bleeding farce, wasn't it? This place is like a bleeding lunatic asylum' Angus's internal telephone rang. He hesitated for a few rings, uncertain whether to answer, then suddenly grabbed-up the handset. 'Angus Taylor,' he boldly, almost challengingly announced, naturally expecting the caller to be none other than his certifiably paranoid employer.

'Hello, Angus.' The cool voice of Stephanie Hargreave pleasantly surprised him; her smooth Canadian accent always thrilled him. 'Could you go to Mr. Mercer's office? He wants to see you immediately,' she calmly asked, unaware of any impending acrimony between Angus and her employer.

Angus's stomach tightened.

'Oh hell, here it comes,' he muttered. It never augured well when Humphrey Mercer summoned anyone through his PA. It was a sure sign of trouble, and Angus entertained thoughts of telling him where he could stuff his job. Despite this young-blooded bravado, however, he preferred not to join the ranks of the unemployed quite so soon and would just have to bend with the expected hail of verbal abuse meted out by this arrogant and strutting martinet.

'If anyone wants me, I'm with HM,' Angus informed his office mate as he left the room.

Humphrey Mercer, better known by his colleagues as HM, was the managing director and main shareholder of Marketing & Advertising Dynamics - more commonly referred to as M&AD. He had failed, or refused to recognise the negative acronym the company name's initial letters created, he being the author of this bizarre appellation. A pedant and self assumed expert on most things - if not everything, Humphrey Mercer preferred to believe that the *thrusting and aggressive image* his company name conveyed was good for business. He dismissed any disparaging comment the name might elicit as *the ravings of madness* and justifiably, many people drew parallels between him and the mental condition the capital letters suggested.

Angus Taylor arrived at his boss's office and was beginning to experience an increase in his anger as he firmly knocked on the panelled door. He entered without waiting for a reply, bursting in to find his employer pacing the carpet his face shrivelled with fury. The cool morning light flashed across the top of HM's smooth, shiny, unnaturally reddish-brown hair as his pale blue eyes bulged at this casually attired copywriter.

'Are you quite out of your mind?' he screamed. 'You know I should fire you for this. What the hell do you think would happen if this got into the hands of one of our clients, eh?' Humphrey Mercer's pulse was in overdrive, his face an over-ripe tomato about to explode, as he flapped the offending flysheet in the air.

'You mean we've still got clients?' Angus flippantly quipped.

'Yes, and with no thanks to you or your damned insolence!' HM shrieked as he ripped the poster into strips and threw them at the floor. 'Your property, I believe. Pick it up and get out before I kick you out!'

'No, no, that's alright, you keep it and with my compliments,' Angus struggled against the rising pressure of suppressed anger within him. 'I thought this was supposed to be a professional advertising agency, not bloody Fawlty Towers!'

HM was by now fissionable. 'Th' the chairman shall hear of th' this irresponsible attitude!' he spluttered with a shrill squeal.

'Ha, ha, the Chairman. You mean *if* he's sober!'

The Besting of Humphrey Mercer

Angus's derisive reply detonated HM's atomic rage. 'You're fired! You can collect a month's money from accounts now and get out at five-thirty, you insufferable semi-literate skinhead!'

'Five-thirty? You really would try to squeeze every last second out of me wouldn't you. You'd even bill your own mother for giving birth to you if you could. I doubt that anyone will have a job by the time you and Angela Bottomly have finished fucking everything up. You couldn't even manage a game of tiddlywinks in a kindergarten!' Angus raged.

Humphrey Mercer's mouth frothed, his face whitened like a chalk cliff. He suddenly growled, moved forward and threw a wild punch at this impudent employee now framed in the open doorway. Angus nimbly ducked back and slammed the door into HM's face.

Stan Molloy was the Chairman and original founder of the company and at 80ish had become an almost fictional image of M&AD's past, like the faded half-tone portraits of ancient company founders printed on boxes of oatcakes, or on tins of mint humbugs. He rarely appeared in the office and popular notions held that he had an alcohol related problem and had been driven into semi-exile by HM's double-crossing, which had relieved him of his controlling shareholding. Such notions were entirely accurate.

HM had uncovered certain irregularities in the way Stan Molloy remunerated himself: untaxed consultancy fees paid to members of his family, a system of claiming expenses for things which did not exist; talents in which HM himself nobly excelled. Stan Molloy, whose daily habit it was to kick-start himself with a pre-lunch bottle of gin, treated this all as fair game, but HM - whose skills in avoiding taxation were fiendishly less obvious - had suggested to Molloy an adjustment in the shareholding to HM's favour, in return for his tactful discretion.

Chapter 2   FLAMES OF INTRIGUE

Hissing with pain and loathing, HM sucked at his bruised knuckles which he'd slammed into the closing door's dense wood panelling. He squeezed his fist hard and squinted into the bright, cold light flaring through his office window, while grinding his teeth. His thoughts drunkenly reeled from one hemisphere of his neural network to the other, desperately trying to re-assemble from a patchwork of seriously impaired recollections, the confusion of events, which had drawn him into this latest humiliation - for which '*She*' was surely responsible.

Angela Bottomly had certainly contributed more than her fair share of ill judgement to recent events, but not without emphatic encouragement from Humphrey Mercer; who in the face of failure would accuse the first person he saw, even if he slipped on his own carelessly discarded banana skin. Metaphorically slipping on banana skins was something he had done much of since Angela had first lifted her stiletto heels across the threshold of Dynamic House.

HM naturally occupied the grandest office on the first floor of the agency's offices, and while he was referred to publicly as HM or Humphrey, other less flattering epithets privately circulated amongst the more lowly paid. A little below average height, HM was a pink and very well-groomed man with a head of thick slicked-back, bottled reddish-brown hair, more city banker in dress than one would expect of an advertising mogul. His whinging and bullying attitude was accompanied by an ego spiked with more than a pinch of self-aggrandisement. He was not one to suffer other people's opinions with any democracy or charity, preferring to bulldoze into the ring his own point of view. Nor did he easily accept new ideas, his earlier military experiences having put paid to any capacity for imagination that he may have once possessed. HM was also tiresomely imbued with a severe passion for punctuality, an obsession which brooked no room for compromise, and on many a dismal rainy morning when the public transport system conspired to abort all hope of passengers arriving at work on time, HM would exercise his employer's prerogative by stationing himself inside the main entrance of M&AD, from where he would challenge the cold and anxious late-comer with a bulge-eyed

The Besting of Humphrey Mercer

stare of indignation while jabbing a manicured finger at his solid gold Longines wristwatch - himself having arrived in the comfort of a chauffeur driven Bentley.

His short tempered rantings, fuelled by a little too much malt whisky, were often sparked by the imagined sabotage of his business by all around him: the spike-haired post room boy was swindling him out of thousands of pounds; every keen executive who took work home was either up to something or a fool; and the well-tempered man an obsequious, devious sycophant.

He was a congenital memorandum writer, the subjects of which were usually thrift: the need to ban private emails, phone calls or post, the shortening of 'coffeebreakslunchhoursmeetings etc.'

In a lighter mood HM could be considered quite charming and generous, especially when in need of a lunch or drinking partner, but to suffer his painfully obscure sense of humour was no small price to pay in return for his hospitality. It took many a glass of good "House Red" to lubricate the throat of a reluctant volunteer before he or she could feign amusement with any real conviction.

Angela Bottomly however, was one person who perversely found no difficulty in enjoying HM's company.

The short, pneumatically endowed Angela was HM's personally recommended addition to the creative team of M&AD and her plump physical geometry - which she skilfully squeezed into some very provocative apparel - succeeded in arousing the baser instincts in her employer, a situation she lost no haste in exploiting. Within a number of weeks less than the number of years Jery Hewitt had served as the creative director of M&AD, Angela had been promoted as his deputy, a decision pressed upon Jery by HM and one which he very reluctantly approved. Jery's agreement was coerced with great difficulty and only on the most emotional of affirmations by HM that if Angela once failed to live up to expectation by so much as a jot during her probationary period, she would be instantly dismissed.

A man of little malice Jery Hewitt's amiable Australian face belied a sharp and alert mind. He could quickly detect the merest whiff of bullshit from 200 yards - an attribute Angela found positively intimidating, fancying herself a master of persuasive rhetoric.

She disliked him from the outset.

Angela's quick and ready espousal of her own brilliance made for an uneasy relationship between herself and her many new co-employees.

The relationship was further aggravated by Humphrey Mercer's creeping obsession with this highly ambitious young jade.

To become a leading voice within the decision making elite of M&AD was Angela's goal, and the manipulation of HM along with any other tactics - foul or even fouler - to advance her cause would be without compromise. She had no respect for Jery and a key move in her ambition would be to take his job. But she was in no hurry; she had time to think her moves through, and sensing a smouldering antipathy between Jery and HM, would carefully contrive to fan the brooding embers into flame.

It wasn't all TV shoots in exotic locations, improbably best lager beers, or meaningless, expensive computer graphics at M&AD. Much of the business profile was, in polite-speak, down-to-earth - despite attempts to win more glamorous clients. High in rank within M&AD's portfolio stood Pearson's Herbal Health Teas - a family business since 1920.

Mr Pearson senior could not, by any stretch of the imagination, be considered the most couth and sophisticated of people to do business with. He described himself often as a man who knew what he liked, declaring that he would know if he liked it when he saw it. Many a copywriter surfaced shell-shocked from a meeting with Pearson senior after he'd turned down yet another ingenious copyline in favour of *"something his wife had thought up"*. Art directors suffered less criticism as Mr Pearson senior usually *"quite liked the pitchers"*.

But such indignities heaped upon those skilled in their particular expertise drew scant sympathy from HM. Pearson paid his fees regularly and on time, a far more important factor than concerns of creative integrity or tweaking the sensitivities of some over-sensitive wordsmith.

As a result, most of the creative department were suddenly and unaccountably busy if a project for Pearson's came in their direction, such was the enthusiasm this account engendered. Jery couldn't even rely on the support of his new deputy Angela, who was usually conveniently closeted in an important meeting with the managing director, a meeting of no real purpose, in Jery's view, other than to provide a sex-starved old roué with the opportunity to strut and pose in front of a fawning, female ingratiate.

Few were ever as enthusiastic over a Pearson's project as good old dependable Reginald Pewsey. This jolly and past his sell-by-date layout artist thrived on sketching-out adverts for strange products. He could

The Besting of Humphrey Mercer

neatly execute pencilled illustrations to accommodate groaningly trite headlines, and those jumbled regurgitations of words once called copy; the incomprehensible result of Pearson senior's inept meddling. The copywriter would have long abandoned all hope of ever being allowed to write original, compelling, or literate English.

'Lovely!' Reg Pewsey would enthuse, briskly rubbing his palms together on receiving such a task. 'I'll knock the little bleeder out in no time!' Naturally enough, he was held in very high esteem by the junior suits, usually assigned to the task of overseeing these less than popular projects.

Much to the amusement of his younger associates, Reg, who vehemently eschewed the use of a computer, would perch himself on a high draughtsman's stool and hunch his solid upper torso over a large drawing board in a small corner office, while manipulating a neatly sharpened lead graphite pencil. His talented little renderings of figures in strange undergarments, adorning his pin-board, stood testimony to the fact that he had been taught to draw properly.

But he also possessed a talent, which was decidedly not appreciated by many of his female colleagues.

Chapter 3   THE ABUSED ABUSE

Most of the lesser-paid workforce at M&AD had ambitions to escape the uncertain sanity of their employer by acquiring a position within a more glamorous advertising agency, and once in a while someone would succeed. Such an event would require the ecstatic candidate to host a "leaving bash", which characteristically involved the unbridled consumption of "house plonk" at a nearby wine bar.

It was during such bacchanalian revelries that the alcoholically charged Reginald Pewsey would undergo a Jekyllian metamorphosis. With his thick topping of white wavy hair, Reg looked good and healthy for his advanced years. He had a disarmingly boyish glint in his blue eyes which rapidly degraded to a bleary-eyed leer when over stimulated by injudicious imbibing. His uncontrollable fingers were irresistibly drawn to the bosom and backside of any young lady who stood within his eager grasp - the younger the better. Those who knew him well usually took his wine-inspired fondling in good spirit. 'Just a bit of innocent fun,' he would declare with a gravely cackle, but those unaccustomed to his over intoxicated proclivities were soon to be sharply surprised at the level of intimacy his "bit of innocent fun" could aspire to.

During his drunken lechery Reg always succeeded in committing what most men could find themselves facing a magistrate for, simply because many dismissed his groping as the flirting of a "harmless old chap". Those women spared his attentions laughed readily but uneasily at his antics, more from relief at not having been singled out. Reg's meek, wide-eyed gasp of disbelief and astonishment when later reminded of his bad behaviour caused many to wonder if his apparent memory loss was as profound as he would have them believe.

Angela Bottomly was one woman, however, whom Reg steered well clear of.

When Angela was fourteen Reg Pewsey was in a relationship with her mother Beatrice and was at her house often. He lavished much attention on both mother and daughter: taking them to the cinema; on sunny-weather trips to the coast; or out for drives in the country. They were a happy little group and outwardly appeared quite the model family.

The Besting of Humphrey Mercer

Reg's own marriage had foundered and Beatrice's husband had succumbed to the enticements of another woman when Angela was still at primary school. Beatrice worked for a company which required her occasional absence from home to attend conferences, but this was never a problem since Reg was always on hand to stay at the house and look after Angela.

During Beatrice's absences however, certain activities took place between Angela and Reg, which matured into more than just innocent displays of affection. Encouraged by Angela's enthusiastic coercion, Reg eventually committed offences of an imprisonable nature. Beatrice's realisation of what had been occurring precipitated such a cataclysmic showdown that only Angela's appeals on Reg's behalf prevented him from spending a long time at Her Majesty's pleasure. Beatrice was also fearful of losing her daughter - on the advice of some high-minded social worker - to the care of an institution where opportunities for child abuse might be even greater.

The relationship was instantly terminated.

Despite the embarrassment of being unwittingly re-united at M&AD, Angela and Reg managed to keep their past depravities securely locked in the closet. They outwardly appeared not to have known each other before affecting a professional but distant relationship throughout the working day. Reg would never look directly at Angela's face, turning his head away if they should ever be in one another's company, fearing in his mind that she might expose him as a pervert and child molester. Sensing his anxiety, Angela revelled in the power it gave her over him, her once infatuation for Reg had turned to one of cynical loathing. She'd have this old ram who'd so vilely molested her.

But all in good time.

The ground floor of M&AD boasted a canopied entrance leading into a tastefully appointed reception area, from which ascended a wide curving stairway. A small lift elevated its cargo of stair-weary souls to the higher levels, but this constantly serviced contraption of dubious reliability, which had occasionally trapped a victim between floors with an inebriated Reg, encouraged sensible women to happily climb the gradually steepening stairway.

Opposite the stairway, panelled double doors opened into a splendid moulded ceilinged hospitality room, which in earlier times had been a small ballroom. Some of the fitted wall mirrors still survived and two sets of French windows opened out to a courtyard.

The basement contained a kitchen and a conference room. From the kitchen refreshment was prepared, including tea or coffee in china cups *for visitors and directors only*. The rest of the staff were obliged to obtain their beverage from the coffee machine near the toilets, a lumbering, steel, floor-standing box displaying twelve grimy push-buttons. These well-soiled plastic switches with their near unreadable titles promised to serve tea, coffee, soup or chocolate in a variety of preferred combinations, but the mixture which this unreliable hulk of technological incompetence dispensed, defied appropriate description in the conventional way. Needless to say, many of those who did avail themselves of this facility were soon inspired to find a suitably unconventional analogy for the scalding chemical travesty deposited into their plastic cup.

'Well it's hot, it's wet, and it's for free' the less discerning would often quote in a feeble attempt at humour.

A long, slate-grey table surrounded by black leather swivel armchairs dominated the basement conference room. At one end of the room hung a projection screen, in front of which stood a lectern, and beside the entrance door an impressive array of switches bristled from a panel which operated various spotlights scattered across the room's ceiling.

This was the very room in which the farcical pitch to the Swedish paint manufacturers had taken place, the gigantic blunder for which HM and Angela had become so deservedly lampooned.

Chapter 4 — Piggleford's Pie

For an obsessive egotist, uncharacteristically, HM harboured a great deal of respect for M&AD's marketing director Digby Hope, and despite his own sense of self-importance placed much trust in this man who held great sway with many of the agency's clients. He saw Digby as his comrade and ally in the "cut and thrust of this aggressive business", not that Digby reciprocated the notion, nor did he expend any energy espousing HM's cause - being sympathetic to the majority of opinion that he was unhinged. Digby Hope, with his head of wire-wool grey hair, silk ties and Armani suits, had a professorial air about him. His tastes in food and wine were profoundly more sophisticated than those of his fellow director and MD.

Some months before the event which was to change his life, HM summoned Digby to his large office and announced plans for them both to visit the premises of Eustace Piggleford, a sausage and pie manufacturer who languished somewhere in the depths of the Somerset countryside. It was an event, which would serve Digby's passion for dining table anecdotes for years to come, and one which contributed to the humiliating event Angus's poster had so justly mocked at the cost of his job.

HM had made the acquaintance of Eustace Piggleford at a golfing event, and having sussed out the possibility of establishing a profitable contact, suggested that Digby and he meet Eustace Piggleford to check out this wealthy food magnate's enterprise, new business being urgently high on M&AD's agenda.

'But this is Malcolm's department,' Digby protested. 'He's the new business executive. Get *him* onto it, that's what he's paid for!'

Malcolm Campbell Patterson had previously joined M&AD as an "aggressive new business go-getter" whose job it was to seek out and secure much needed new clients, but it had become clearer and clearer each month that he was go-getting nowhere fast. Malcolm had been employed against Digby's advice by HM, who now reluctantly had to accept the mistake he'd made.

'To hell with Malcolm!' HM spat back. You and me, I want you and me to check this one out.' He walked over to his desk, briskly slid out a deep bottom drawer and drew out a plastic carrier bag containing a selection of out-of-sell-by-date pork pies. 'I've managed to get hold of some of Piggleford's product for research purposes,' he whispered in mock secrecy. 'I'm getting the creative bods to come up with some new and more up-to-date package designs, and I'm also organising a tasting session with the staff this evening in the old ballroom. This'll give us the chance to find out what people really think of Piggleford's pies.' HM tossed a couple of pork pies onto his desktop. They smacked the teak surface like two segments of rock, and Digby frowned when he saw for the first time, the tasteless pig logo skipping above the factory's address - Happy-Hog Farm.

The general opinion of the agency staff was one of profoundly disrespectful negativity. 'To call this a load of old tripe would be an insult to offal!' George Birtles from the production department had dared to quip during the pie tasting. HM silently fumed at George Birtle's frivolity and made a mental note that George would be the next in line for some cruel punishment, some particularly nasty task which would humiliate and harry this ordinary family man whose life depended on his job. The snake pit of HM's vindictiveness was fathomless when plumbed. He seemed to take a perverse glee in *winding up* lesser-paid employees, persons over whom he had a certain power of livelihood. Naturally enough, HM declined to pass an opinion of the pie himself and took but the merest nibble with a generous gulp of the red wine he had laid on as a means of coercing those present into participating in this after-work-hours, gastronomic orgy, an episode Angela had excused herself from on the grounds that "she was not feeling awfully, terribly well".

For a factory described by Eustace Piggleford as "just 15 minutes from the station", he and Digby were buffeted in their taxi for an uncomfortably long time as it rumbled down endless tree laden, bird whistling, country lanes in the afternoon summer sun. Cow parsley bowed in hedgerows, teasel rocked stiffly and sparrows exploded from hawthorn as the elderly hearse-like saloon "licensed to carry passengers" lumbered by on its eternal journey. Heavenly though the landscape was, Digby wondered how long it would be before he could tope a cool gin and tonic, assuming a half decent hostelry existed in this rural backwater.

The Besting of Humphrey Mercer

HM and Digby were scheduled to meet Eustace Piggleford, sole proprietor of Piggleford's, which had once been described by the late Mr. Piggleford senior, "as purveyors of the finest pork pies and sausages to the carriage trade". This was back in the days before the business had moved south from a farm in the Yorkshire dales; when the product was considered to be good.

Digby was to be of a less biased opinion.

After an introductory meeting with Eustace Piggleford, HM and Digby would take in a full tour of the pie and sausage-making plant the following day. The plan was for them both to stay as guests of Mr. and Mrs. Piggleford at their new residence in the village of Tilting Green, a prospect which invoked no joy in Digby.

'It's no inconvenience at all Humphrey, you can stay with us no problem,' Eustace Piggleford had enthused as he offered the two admen a bed. 'It saves money on hotels and that, apart from which there's not much in the way of accommodation near the factory anyway!' he confirmed to a delighted HM during a telephone conversation to finalise this investigative trip. Digby was not delighted at being denied the comfort of a hotel and was still of the opinion that Malcolm Campbell Patterson should be making this tedious trip, however useless he might be. After all, this was precisely what he was being paid to do.

'Factory? Place looks more like a concentration camp,' Digby murmured when the taxi at last approached the gates of "Happy Hog Farm home of Piggleford's Pork Products", as the legend on the large curved signboard spanning the gate informed its visitors. 'Oh Gawd look! They've even got that dreadful logo above the gate,' he groaned with disdain and loathing. HM hissed at him to be quiet. The reviled logo took the form of a giant cut-out painted pig, dressed in top hat and tails, grinning and prancing on hind legs, a monocle screwed into one of its piggy eyes. With a garland of sausages about its neck, the burlesque porcine parody brandished a butcher's cleaver and frying pan in white-gloved humanoid hands. Its sinister, rouged-cheeks and slit-eyed leer seemed to be appraising the new visitors' suitability for dismemberment and mincing into pie filling. A long lashed squint-eye seemed to wink at Digby, and he shuddered.

This archaic trademark had been the subject of much earlier dissonance when Digby was airing his opinion on new package designs at HM's pie-tasting evening.

'That hideous pig should go for a start!' Digby opined and most of those present agreed.

'I-it-it's the company trade mark, for God's sake!' HM spluttered. 'They've had it for damn near sixty years now so I think *you* should think more carefully before making remarks like that!' HM tried to lower the pitch of his shrill croaking, looking wildly about him, seemingly in expectation of the pig suddenly jumping through a window to hack Digby into joints with its cleaver. The others sighed with despair at this unnecessarily petulant outburst and none more so than the two art directors, Susanne Vérdier and Dean Dalton, who'd been ordered by HM to work on this project. Normally it would be Jery's decision to select the appropriate creative team, but in HM's opinion this dismissal of good manners would save time, after all *he* was the boss and this was *his* project. Good manners rarely applied to HM. He'd wanted Angela Bottomly involved but she had excused herself on the grounds that it would be more appropriate to call on her particular talents when a proper creative advertising campaign was needed. A project as lowly and uncouth as writing the words for package designs was decidedly absent from the self-aggrandising fiction, which constituted her curriculum vitae. The involvement, advice or even general opinion of Malcolm Campbell Patterson was not remotely up for consideration - to his bitter chagrin.

'Hang on, I'm sorry, Humphrey, but I thought you said our brief was to give Piggleford's packaging a new and up-to-date image!' Digby argued.

HM grimaced, sucked breath through clenched teeth and screamed, 'Yes, but it doesn't mean that we've got to bloody well dump their logo!' He calmed and continued with a whimper of resignation, 'We're on a tight enough budget as it is.'

'Budget? You've never mentioned budget. Surely someone has to decide whether the business is worth pursuing before we commit to any expenditure,' Digby shouted. 'Isn't that what we're supposed to be paying Campbell Patterson for?'

HM's face became a study in puce, his eyes bulging to the point of rupture. 'I think I am quite capable of deciding whether or not the business is worth pursuing,' he squealed with indignity. 'We don't want to scare the client off by exposing him to Campbell bloody Patterson who doesn't know his arse from his elbow! Let him loose with the costings and we'll end up losing a small fortune!'

'Well, you hired him,' Digby casually followed with a shrug of the shoulders. HM sighed, walked over to one of the large French windows

The Besting of Humphrey Mercer

and stared vacantly out at the melancholy evening sky. The sun was an orange ember dying somewhere on the horizon among dark, tattered strips of cloud. He would often become quiet and introspective after one of his juvenile outbursts, as if attempting to becalm his thumping pulse and stave off a possible heart attack. Most of those present uncharitably wished he'd have one, preferably fatal.

After an uneasy silence, HM walked slowly to his chair with fingers knotted behind his back, his face wearing the expression of a tortured and long suffering martyr. He adopted a patronising tone as he sat down in front of his plate of barely nibbled Piggleford's pie, took a swig of wine, and revealed his strategy.

'It's a sprat to catch a mackerel,' he almost whispered. 'We do a good job on Piggleford's packaging designs, then we go for his *above-the-line* advertising budget. Get him onto TV and into the big supermarket chains, even if it means losing money on the first project. He makes other things besides pork pies, you know,' HM concluded, tapping the side of his nose with a blunt forefinger, while exposing the conceited smile of one who knows more than he has revealed. This non-strategy created deep suspicion within the others, but it was not contested since HM was the only person to have had dialogue with Eustace Piggleford so far.

At the golf club dinner where HM and Eustace Piggleford first met, they discovered that they had both done time in the same regiment, and during the enthusiastic conversation which followed HM suggested - rather more than Eustace had requested - a professional review of his company's packaging, explaining that new package designs would enhance his company's position in the market place, would lead to a significant increase in sales, and of course, how well qualified M&AD was to handle such a challenge. HM further claimed that it "would not cost much" to do an advertising campaign either, but such an assertion was usually the prelude to a very high invoice from M&AD, and Eustace suspected this might be the case. However he did warm to the idea a bottle of Armagnac later, courtesy of HM, and eventually became positively ecstatic about it; after all, an ex-army man wouldn't rip off another ex-army man, ex-warrant officer Eustace Piggleford persuaded himself.

'Er, excuse me, Humphrey, but according to the advertising registers Piggleford has never made any advertising expenditure in the past, above or below-the-line. I mean, has he got the production capacity and the distribution network to enter into the supermarkets? It would be very unwise to produce TV advertising for a product which might not be able to meet consumer demands,' Eve Merrell, the irritatingly sensible media planner, reasoned.

'Exactly!' Digby shouted. 'They're hardly *Walls* or *Mr Kipling's*, are they? No-one's ever heard of them, and judging by our overwhelming enthusiasm for the product, their pies are hardly likely to be a sell-out!'

HM leaned back in his chair writhing. He interlocked his fingers, squeezed his hands together and stared at the ceiling, his thin moustached mouth stretched into a buckled grimace. He might have been praying, the others could but wonder. He jumped to his feet, his fist thumping the table and rounded on Digby. 'That's why I want *you* and me to check it out dammit,' his beetroot face creased with anger, 'not that zombie, Campbell Patterson!'

Beyond the gates of Happy Hog Farm, languished a clutter of old concrete one-level buildings and a 16th century barn, which had been tastefully re-roofed in red-rusted corrugated iron. Eustace Piggleford pushed back windblown strips of sparse yellow hair from his small swede-head and smiled enthusiastically as he met HM and Digby disembarking from their taxi. He shook hands vigorously and Digby noted the frayed cuffs of his host's well-worn tweed jacket. His grimy tie was of some military stripe and contrasted unpleasantly with his bile-coloured poplin shirt. Scuffed, sturdy brown brogues stuck out from the narrow bottoms of his fawn cavalry twill trousers, revealing an alarmingly long pair of feet, putting Digby in mind of an old music hall act - he couldn't recall the name.

'So the heavy mob have arrived at last!' Eustace announced on noting Digby's smart fashionable attire, and it was clear to Digby that he was gazing upon the grubby demeanour of a wealthy and parochial cheapskate.

"Tears for souvenirs h'that's h'what yeeou've left me..." The strains of an archaic and familiar song slid along the breeze from the PA system as the door to one of the buildings opened and closed for a white ghost-faced pastry maker who'd stepped out for a quick cigarette. After a couple of long blissful drags the ghost spotted Eustace and his guests walking into the yard, and quickly dematerialised before being seen.

'Had the tiles off that for our new house,' Eustace boasted pointing to the vandalised, listed barn as he walked HM and Digby towards two new Portakabins.

'Local council didn't object then?' Digby casually commented.

The Besting of Humphrey Mercer

'I don't know, and quite frankly I don't give a bloody monkey's whether the buggers object or not. I'm certainly not going to ask their permission either. I'll do what I want with my own property!' Eustace declared, with defensive and swelling pride.

'Well quite,' Digby answered, with seemingly no more concern for the building's mutilation than that of his host's opinion.

Adjacent to the Portakabins lay a long flat-roofed, old concrete building with a small quality control laboratory at one end. The lab was manned by an overworked and underpaid biochemist, with an ancient LC analyser. His hair-tearing job was to keep the authorities satisfied that the required amount of vitamin and preservative levels were being maintained in Piggleford's pies and sausages, and that a less than lethal quantity of fat and chemicals met the minimum EC standards. This, in Eustace Piggleford's opinion, was a time-wasting and unnecessary expense foisted on him by interfering busybody foreign bureaucrats.

'Good old British homemade country cooking,' was how Eustace described Piggleford's pies. 'None of your organic nonsense here, and who needs all that hygiene business anyway? It's not natural. Nothing wrong with a bit of clean honest dirt. Gives it more flavour.' These views were often expressed to Suresh Vakram the long-suffering biochemist. Suresh suffered nightmares over Eustace's profoundly casual attitude towards standards of cleanliness in food production. But suffering of a bacterial variety was something that a number of the less alert staff at Piggleford's became intimately acquainted with. They were those gullible souls who unwisely took advantage of Eustace Piggleford's "generosity". Friday afternoon was that one and only day of the week he would encourage staff to take home any leftover pies or sausages as a little perk, as he saw it. 'Get some decent grub in your belly this weekend,' he would exhort an unsuspecting cleaner or packer, about to dispose of under baked pies or reject sausages.

Eustace Piggleford's office in the new Portakabin was a symphony in brown: a brown desk, brown leather swivel chair, brown carpet and two brown fake wood-grained filing cabinets. He politely motioned HM and Digby to the brown tweed-seated visitors' chairs regimentally aligned in front of his desk.

'You're in a bit of a brown study then?' HM quipped followed by red-faced, nervous horse laughter.

'Eh! You what?' Eustace bleated as he blankly looked up from his brown leather desk diary. A faint knock on the door stilled them all and a frightened-faced lady entered the room wearing clear plastic overshoes, a small white plastic trilby hat and a white linen coat bearing the embroidered emblem of a prancing pig on its lapel.

"Tears for souvenirs..." The faint crooning voice followed her in as she fearfully clutched a tray on which sat three china cups of tea chattering in their saucers along with three large, carefully sliced wedges of Piggleford's jumbo pork pie.

'I thought you'd be a little peckish after your long journey,' said Eustace, rubbing his hands with juvenile delight. 'Go on, get it down yer.' Digby's hopes of a cool gin and tonic faded away like the retreating, shuffling timid tea lady. The pork pie predictably lived up to Digby's expectation with its dubious contents encased in cold rock-hard pastry, which was as dry as sawdust when it finally yielded to molar. The crunch of gristle caused him to have a serious problem with his stomach. Eustace enthusiastically pushed pie into his mouth like an uncoordinated chimpanzee at a tea party.

'Now go on tell me truly,' he demanded, his voice muffled by the combined skills of chewing while speaking. 'You've not tasted anything like that for a long time, I'll bet!'

'Not for a long time,' Digby agreed and surreptitiously spat a lump of gristle into his paper napkin.

'Yes, it's er, rather good,' HM weakly suggested. Digby tried to kick him in the ankle but only succeeded in dropping pie into his teacup. It was too late, the damage was done.

'Debsie, could you come in please!' Eustace called out towards a little office across the small corridor within Eustace's shouting range. Debsie swiftly appeared beaming at the visitors. 'Get some more pie in, love. These gennelmen are half starved, and get Mr Hope some fresh tea. He got so carried away he's dropped pie into it.'

'Oh no please don't trouble yourself,' Digby protested as he spooned soggy dollops of pastry from his teacup, only to have his sentence cut short by Eustace.

'Don't be daft. It's no trouble, is it Debsie!' he spat, with pie crumbs flying from his mouth. Debsie looked down to Digby, her cleavage bubbling from a deep V-necked sweater, and grinned in a most peculiar manner, her head oscillating from side to side.

'No trouble at all, sir.'

Of generous proportions, Debsie wasn't unattractive, but her eyes had a strange squint which unnerved Digby a little. She had never had the pleasure of meeting top London advertising executives before and was fascinated by their cool worldly manner and nice suits; as she would later report to her mother. Her mother took a healthy interest in men of any shape, race, or religion whom her daughter took an interest in, provided they were well heeled.

The factory was closing down for the day. Teacups and tray were cleared and Eustace leaned back in his chair, chewing the faded black stem of a pipe between his crooked, tobacco-stained teeth. He both spoke and sucked, causing the charred bowl to eject crackling sparks and thick convolutions of blue aromatic smoke into the room, as if fearing this wheezing, sizzling Vesuvius might die if not continually coaxed.

The meeting, though amicable, had gone on long enough to HM's tiring mind, and there was not much more to say that couldn't be said over a drink, so he abandoned himself to a hopelessly desperate gambit. Looking at his watch in mock disbelief he stood up.

'Good Lord it's six thirty already,' HM gasped. 'We've kept you late and we've taken up far too much of your valuable time. If you know of a good pub somewhere, let us buy you a drink, or perhaps you'd let us take you and Mrs Piggleford out for dinner tonight. We could phone her and she could meet us!' Digby grinned, nodding his agreement with an expression of enthusiasm bordering on hysteria. Eustace stared hypnotically into middle space, nodding his head slowly from side to side, his finger tamping down the cindered shag expiring in his curved Peterson briar.

'No, no, Humphrey, there's nothing around these parts. Sit down and relax lad,' Eustace murmured. 'It's all in hand. She'll be here any moment now.' He pulled open a desk drawer and placed the now extinguished pipe inside. HM and Digby exchanged quizzing glances and Eustace continued, 'The other half, she's meeting us in the Mercedes and taking us all home for supper, a damn fine cook she is too' the enthusiastic voice dropped to a whisper directed from the side of Eustace's handlebar moustached mouth, 'but be a bit careful with the booze. She can get a bit y'know.' He noted Digby's drooping countenance and lightened up. 'Don't get me wrong I like a drop myself, but I'm a little careful when Sheila's around, she's likely to become... well, y'know, very emotional.'

Chapter 5   Sheila takes a Plunge

Sheila Piggleton was an ex-showgirl of sorts, fortyish, aspiring middle-class with a contrived county accent, which was betrayed by her dodgy diction. Save for an unnaturally black and stiff hairdo she was quite attractive, dressed very expensively, and fairly dripped with precious jewellery. But somehow she still managed to look a little cheap.

Tilting Green was a 30 minute drive away and proved very dreary for a country village, consisting of a scattering of houses along a single street, a small general store, a tiny spit and sawdust pub - where the local yokels slaked their hay-choked thirsts with warm cider or stale beer, while discussing hoof paring and foot rot - a newsagent and "*Uppercut*", a unisex hairdresser. At the end of this motley trail of traders stood a small stone-built bank defiantly flying a tattered Union Jack, like the last outpost of some distant colony.

'Stop here a minute, Sheil,' Eustace called as the bank slid into view. 'I've just got to pop something in the bank!' He stepped from the parked car's open door with a plastic carrier bag, which he'd been nursing between his knees during the journey.

'Woss that then!' Sheila enquired with sharp disapproval.

'Oh, it's just 'is nibbs' sausages,' Eustace reluctantly affirmed. He turned and smiled to the two passengers in the back of the Mercedes. 'It's for the bank manager. He'll be right choked off if he doesn't get these for his breakfast.' Digby and Rod watched open mouthed while Eustace pushed a pound of Piggleford's pork sausages through the bank's large letterbox.

'Don't know why he can't buy his own bloomin' sossidges!' Sheila sighed. 'He makes quate enough money off of us as it is.'

'It's wise to keep y' bank manager sweet,' Eustace commented directly to Digby and Rod, rather than answer his wife.

Down a long concrete drive stood the recently built Piggleford residence, incongruously roofed with the clay peg tiles purloined from the noble barn to which they had originally belonged. The architecture was a travesty of pseudo Spanish-Americana on a split-level format with

The Besting of Humphrey Mercer

an arched colonnaded driveway to the main entrance. On a plinth beside the front door stood a wrought iron prancing pig holding a painted wooden sign displaying the name "Sows Rest".

'Sheila thought that one up,' Eustace proudly boasted as his two London guests mentally vomited.

HM and Digby stood in the reception room with yet another cup of weak tea which had just been served them by Peg, the home help, maid, or whatever she needed to be. The large capable, early sixties Peg, readily displayed a warm and friendly smile.

'Mr & Mrs Piggleford are just changing and will be with you shortly,' she told them on removing the tea vessels. HM and Digby had been shown to their very comfortably appointed guest room with, mercifully, two single beds and after a quick wash and brush-up were admiring the garden from the floor-to-ceiling windows of this mock Spanish room with its whitewashed walls, yellow and white ceramic tiled floor and cow hide furniture. The large sliding windows opened onto a patio and swimming pool tiled to match those in the room. The garden was beautifully laid out in a traditionally English style, the landscaping being very classical and mature. They could only speculate that this architectural abomination had been built upon the ruins of some previous more glorious dwelling, which - due to Eustace's lack of concern for preservation as evidenced by his attitude to the barn - had been razed to the ground in order to build the out-of-character pile, which now sat in the ancient grounds.

Behind them, Digby noted with anticipatory glee, was a bar. Three wrought iron, basket-seated stools stood in front of the counter. Digby scanned the assorted bottles stacked neatly on the shelves behind and noted, to his crushing vexation, that there was not a single drop of gin.

'Right then, gentlemen, I think we all need a little aperitif before supper!' Sheila Piggleford commanded as she sashayed across the room heavily perfumed and wearing an expensive black sequinned cocktail dress. Eustace, attired in what could only be termed as dull department store casual, trotted at her heel silently opening and closing his mouth in protestation. 'Now we've got sweet or medium dray Cyprus sherry, or perhaps you'd lake a little Sinzzano.' Sheila lifted bottles and glasses down from the shelf. 'Or would you prefer a little shampers? I'm sure Eustace has got some stashed in the cellar, eh Dear?' Digby's eyes blinked like a newly illuminated Christmas tree; he liked this woman already.

'Er, no Dear,' Eustace replied with strangled irritation, 'not now. It won't be properly chilled anyway, that's if we've got any left!'

'You wouldn't have a cold beer would you?' HM optimistically enquired.

'Tut! tut! beer? I thought you advertising types went in for more sophisticated drinks than beer. You would 'aff t' be awkward, don't think that we've got any beer,' Sheila Piggleford groaned as she stooped down behind the bar's counter. Eustace leapt in glowing with sudden enthusiasm.

'I'll get Peg to see if there's any in the kitchen, Dear!' he trilled in a triumphant tone.

'No there issn't, Stacey! And Peg's puttin' the final touches to dinner, so keep out of the kitchin. If you can't find one measly bottle of bubbly then I'm sure these gentlemen will be quate 'appy with somethink we've got here,' Sheila Piggleford firmly responded, with a prickliness that betrayed intense irritation. She knelt to rummage in the bar's little fridge. 'No beer in here,' she sighed, wobbling on stiletto heels. She slipped as she rose up and Digby deftly caught her in his arms.

'Thank you, sir,' Sheila said, as she sweetly smiled, and Digby paid Sheila the most oily and fawning of compliments, perhaps a little over-the-top to HM's mind. Digby's experience had taught him that half the battle in winning new contracts is in making sure one gets on well with the client's wife. As Sheila stood, the warm glow from a large lamp on the bar dramatically caught her face in a half-light.

'Sheila, I must say you look stunning,' Digby exhaled in a ludicrously suave voice. 'You're the image of that beautiful woman in the T.V. commercials, isn't she, Humphrey!' he called to his MD, and continuing his line in slime took a hand and helped her to a bar stool cooing, 'Come, let me pour you a drink. You've been busy enough already.'

HM didn't know which TV commercial Digby was referring to, if indeed any. Eustace looked on puzzled and grim faced. There was a pause, a static moment as the whole universe seemed to stop. Sheila slowly drew up a shapely leg and crossed it over the other.

'I'll have a Sinzzano please, Digby,' she softly murmured, looking into his eyes. The tension in the room slackened, and HM started to breathe again. Digby took up a tall glass and spun it in the air.

'Cinzano it is then. Some ice and soda perhaps?' he suggested, now assured of his standing.

'Well, absolutely!' Sheila giggled, and she let the shoe on the foot of her crossed leg slip and dangle from her big toe. 'Only a teenzy one though, dinner will be served soon.' She turned to Eustace with cold fire in her eyes. 'And I trust we'll be havin' some of your wane with it!' Digby

The Besting of Humphrey Mercer

quickly presented her with a generous measure of expertly prepared Cinzano and soda in the crystal hi-ball, and Sheila took a long slow draught. 'Um, that's gorgeous,' she sighed, and took a second satisfying swig. Digby wondered why Eustace had commented on Sheila's attitude towards drink as she clearly appreciated a tipple, but then Digby was not to know about the devastating effect a small amount of alcohol could have on Sheila. He was more used to the company of his women associates in advertising, who have seen many a drunken boasting male associate under the table.

His mind wandered back to the time when Malcolm Campbell Patterson had first joined M&AD.

One evening Digby and Malcolm, along with a small group from the office, were enjoying a Friday evening drink or two. This agreeable session took place at a nearby wine bar. Flushed and slurring after a boozy lunch and several glasses of Burgundy, Malcolm began to regale Susanne Vérdier with propositions of a lewd and unsubtle nature while constantly topping up her glass. To the immense amusement of the others, Susanne heroically held her own until at last, an over intoxicated Malcolm belched and dribbled red wine down his tasteless tie. Gargling an apology he slowly slid from his chair, slithered to the toilet and spent the rest of the evening *"talking to God on the great white telephone"*; as Jery Hewitt termed Malcolm's alimentary evacuations. Malcolm Campbell Patterson revelled in his full name's initials and wore a tie with the capital letters M.C.P. printed in a repeat pattern interspaced with little pink pigs. Susanne found no difficulty in enjoying much pleasure over this man's humiliation. During Malcolm's absence the others decided to go in search of a Chinese restaurant, and Digby duly went to the lavatory to inform Malcolm. The kneeling supplicant most dramatically declined the offer by howling and burying his head even deeper into the white porcelain lavatory bowl.

Digby was aroused from his reverie by an announcement that dinner was about to be served, and he accompanied Sheila into the dining room. The egg mayonnaise was predictably an egg with a blob of bland, bottled mayonnaise, and Digby's hunger diminished as he sat at the Piggleford's dining table, forking another morsel of cold hard-boiled albumin into his reluctant mouth. HM however, wishing not to insult Sheila, shovelled every last crumb into his stomach.

'Very nice.' HM smiled, as the portly Peg removed the first course crockery from the supper table. She beamed at this smart, well-groomed man, who'd all but scraped the printed wild flower pattern from his plate.

'Have some more wine, Digby,' Eustace blurted, as he spat specks of mayonnaise across the table. Digby was not moved to ecstasy by Eustace's choice of wine either, but was thirsty and grateful for anything which might encourage him to relish the rest of the mediocre banquet about to emerge from the Piggleton's kitchen.

'I do like a glass of good wane with my meal, don't you?' Sheila questioned Digby, her cerise mouth pulled into an odd grin.

'Oh yes! most certainly, as long as it complements the food,' Digby pointedly answered side-spying the label on the wine bottle that was now being proffered.

'Whate wane with whate meat, an' red wane with red meat, served at room temperature: that's my simple rule,' Sheila declared in her strange diction, while stabbing the table top with a long forefinger. Digby swallowed hard while Eustace displayed a look of sour irritation.

'I suppose you got that bloody nonsense from "Harry Krishna",' Eustace mumbled. Sheila inhaled audibly and froze while the two guests remained thoroughly puzzled by the comment.

'Ee doess'nt drink wane,' she spat and turned to face Digby. 'We're havin' chikkin Kiev tonight. Go on then, Stacey, tell them!' Sheila demanded from a red drooping mouth, which had been heavily applied with lipstick. She was beginning to exhibit the florid, voluptuous look of a recently feasted vampire.

'Well, er, it was going to be a surprise.' Eustace inflated his chest like some scrawny rooster and crowed, 'It's one of ours, well, four in fact.' He chuckled at his witticism. 'We're going to be eating Piggleford's "Great Gates Chopped Chicken Kiev" tonight, the first batch from a brand new line we're introducing this autumn; in fact, Humphrey reckons that he could get us on TV with this one. He had this idea of using that Mussorgsky tune, you know, the Gate of Kiev bit, to underline the product's name. Clever, eh? In fact, he even came up with the name for us didn't you, Humphrey.' HM smiled a weak smile while Digby smiled the sick smile of someone mentally strangling Humphrey Mercer, and Eustace continued regaling the table with what he regarded as useful and interesting information. 'We've done a deal with an egg farm over at Wately who've got sheds and sheds loaded to the gunnell's with hundreds of old battery layers. Now, when they're clapped out and stop laying they're useless, no more 'an dog meat see! So we buy them for peanuts, wring their necks and ...'

The Besting of Humphrey Mercer

'Oooh! spare us the details plee-ese, Stay-cee. We are eating them, after all!' Sheila cut in before Digby threw up.

'Oh, sorry. Well, see what you think anyway. I think you'll be quite surprised,' the admonished, red-faced Eustace answered, before draining his wine glass. Peg reappeared and set down four large flower-patterned china dinner plates.

'I think we might stretch to another bottle of wane as well please, Peg, don'chew you think, Digby?' Sheila slurred. 'See if there's any of that nace Chabliss hidden in the scullery!' Eustace was about to protest, but Digby was making such enthusiastic noises of approval that Eustace could only sit and swallow his irritation.

Peg, with the solemn slow dignity of an undertaker, deposited before each of each of them a thirty millimetre thick slab of some orange breadcrumbed material fashioned in the crude cartoon shape of a chicken's leg. Eustace brightened up.

'Look at that then?' he proudly enthused, rubbing his hands together.

'Brussels sprouts, sir?' Peg quietly intoned, as she leaned over HM's shoulder, pressing her large bosom into the side of his head, and bearing a silver serving tray piled high with enough assorted steamed vegetables to feed the entire British Army. Enchanted by this ex-military gentleman, Peg made sure that HM had a goodly serving of everything.

'D'you know, we can stamp a hundred of these out of a one metre slab of rolled chicken gunk?' Eustace attempted to return to his informative commentary. 'And the off cuts go into our chicken and ham pies!' Digby sombrely nodded. 'If they'll eat that they'll eat anything,' Eustace once again ventured at humour.

'Eustace really!' Sheila shrieked spraying a fine rain of wine onto Digby's glasses.

'No, no, only joking, only joking, gentlemen,' Eustace offered as a weak reassurance. 'Actually it's bloody good, even if I say so.'

'Well you'd aff t' say so even if you didn' think so,' Sheila said, her mouth packed with half chewed chicken as she shook with convulsive mirth. Digby smiled wanly and wiped his spectacles, bemused by the design of this ludicrous and unwholesome dish.

'Well, I must say I like a bit of leg myself,' he feebly quipped, and gingerly pushed his fork into the serving of Great Gates Chopped Chicken Kiev. Sheila slapped the table's edge and expelled a high cackling laugh followed by a fit of violent coughing. Eustace jumped from his seat to thump Sheila's back while she choked and spluttered into her napkin.

'That's what comes of yakking and stuffing y' face at the same time,' Eustace observed with restrained anger. Digby thought the remark a little rich coming from a man who spoke while chewing and stabbing his fork towards whomever he was addressing, in a most confrontational manner. Order was restored, and Digby took a mouthful of Piggleford's new product. The texture was of warm stringy rubber, with a stinging aftertaste of some chemical garlic flavour. The old hen meat was so tough that no self-respecting fox would be seen within 20 miles of Happy Hog Farm. The Brussels sprouts were another marvel of modern cuisine, having an ice-cold crunchiness to them that defied reason although Eustace offered one.

'I don't think these sprouts have been cooked long enough!' he called out to Sheila.

'Stacey!' Sheila sharply responded, '*owl denty*, that's how vegetables should be cooked, *owl denty*. If you overcook them you remove all of the vitamins and trace elimints or somethink. An' I got that from Harry Krishna, as you insist on calling him. He told me hisself, an' he should know bein' a *bial* chemist,' she firmly responded, with smug confidence.

'Huh, I wouldn't believe everything he says, if I were you,' Eustace scowled. 'Bio chemist he may be, but you still can't drink the bloody water where he comes from.'

Sheila released squawks of laughter like the short shrieks of a file running across the edge of sheet metal. 'Ooh, your juss' jealous,' she wailed, ''cos 'ees good lookin'.'

Digby, confused by references to Harry Krishna - but not wishing to add fuel to his host's sniping disparagements by enquiring - set off on a line of conversation designed to distract attention from the ghastly meal in front of him. He bewitched his hosts with delightfully amusing anecdotes, occasionally aided by HM, who contributed the odd obscure joke. The ploy worked well. Peg cleared the plates without any of the enthralled company noticing Digby's large quantity of leftover chicken and Brussels sprouts. HM had eaten all of his meal, and Sheila Piggleford had likewise displayed a more than healthy appetite. Sheila's constant laughter emulated the rasping inhalations of someone being strangled as she anticipated the punch lines of HM's more embarrassingly ludicrous funnies.

Back in the reception room, the three men sat in more comfortable chairs, as opposed to the uncomfortable high-backed moulded plastic devices at the dining table.

'I take it we'll all be having coffee,' Eustace asked his guests, and quite suddenly Sheila appeared triumphantly clasping a bottle of fine

The Besting of Humphrey Mercer

Armagnac. Her lipstick had become smeared around her mouth due to the over-enthusiastic application of her table napkin during the dubious event, which passed as dinner. She tripped towards Digby with red stained teeth bared.

'Carmin! d'you like Carmin, Digby?' Sheila's slurring speech was slipping by degrees into a rougher dialect, and Eustace winced with anger and alarm.

'What? Oh Bizet's Carmen you mean.'

'Oooh! Ha ha hee! Sheila,' howled, pouring him brandy and spilling it over his trousers, 'I don't mean Carmin 'air rollers.' She brayed like an epileptic donkey and walked over to HM to pour him a brimming glass of Eustace's expensive vintage as if it were barroom plonk. Eustace was thoroughly put out at this waste of good Armagnac, and desperate to prevent Sheila from embarrassing him any further, gently relieved her of the bottle. He made an announcement in the feeble hope of distracting his wife from her slatternly descent.

'Sheila loves the opera y'know, sings in our local operatic society, don't you, dear? Got a damn fine soprano voice,' he said, with the stiff expression of someone fearing even more embarrassment. HM looked up from his drink and nodded with exaggerated interest. 'Yes, we sometimes have a few friends over and Sheila puts on a little show, on the lawn there by the pool, don't you, love!' Eustace shouted. Sheila raised her glass and threw the expensive Armagnac into the back of her mouth.

Doing exceptionally well to show some interest in a subject which he knew little about, HM politely asked Eustace in his pompous manner. 'What sort of stuff is it Sheila sings then?'

'Oh, you know, songs from the shows er, what'sisname, Lloyd George, bit of Gilbert and Sullivan, that sort of thing.'

'Webber!' Sheila squealed as she slid back the patio doors to let in the fragrant, warm evening air. Chuckling mischievously she left the room. During her absence the distinctive sound of Bizet's popular opera became audible from hidden speakers. The patio was floodlit to deter burglars as well as to afford a view of the garden when night had fallen, and Peg set coffee on the bar counter. Eustace, certain that Sheila had finally succumbed to the wine and gone to bed, launched into a summary of the itinerary for the following day's visit to the factory.

It was during this briefing that Digby saw a movement outside. Eustace and HM were sitting on a long sofa with their backs to the open patio doors, while Digby lounged in an armchair opposite them with a good view of the garden. He clearly saw Sheila Piggleford over at the far side of the large illuminated pool gyrating along the edge with a red silken shawl across her shoulders and clicking castanets in time with Bizet's music, performing what appeared to be a parody of Carmen's dance. She teetered beside the still blue water in her dangerously high-heeled shoes. Digby froze with his mouth locked open; he couldn't speak. As the music crescendoed, Eustace, irritated by the music's rising volume, glanced around to witness his wife's bizarre tomfoolery. He catapulted from his seat through the open patio doors and pranced over to the pool where Sheila was now precariously swaying. Eustace quietly demanded that she desist from making a bloody fool of herself and to stop acting like a stupid tart.

'Piss-off, pimple-head,' Sheila was heard to shout above the music, and a struggle ensued. She clenched a large, castanet-filled hand and caught Eustace a clacking biff in the face. As her fist met the resistance of her husband's eye socket, she momentarily wobbled at the pool's edge wheeling her arms at the night sky in a desperate bid to regain her balance. Eustace, clutching his throbbing eye, made no attempt to help. Sheila grabbed at his waistband and they both fell into the cold water. They surfaced with the red shawl clinging around Sheila's head. Her howls of indignity alarmed HM and Digby and they rose from their seats, only to be stopped by the sight of the capable Peg storming across the lawn from the back of the house. Peg helped Eustace out, and they both dragged Sheila cursing and screaming from the pool. The ridiculously stiff hairdo which had graced Sheila's head at the dinner table, bobbed across the disturbed water. The hysterical stream of expletive-laden invective Sheila spat at Eustace was only silenced by the crack of Peg's flattened palm across the side of her face - an act of restraint she had clearly been called upon to execute many times before. Digby wondered at the relationship between Peg and the Pigglefords, that she could treat her mistress in this way. Deeply embarrassed, HM and Digby quickly finished their fine brandy and retired to their room while Bizet's Carmen continued its lively accompaniment.

Digby thought Sheila's natural short, dark spiky hair, far more attractive than her wig, which had now sunk to the bottom of the pool.

Chapter 6   A REALLY OFFAL LUNCH

The following morning had a dark gloom about it: the sky dull and dripping, the temperature cool. There was no other noise except the continual tattoo of rain on tiles and the giggling of water along gutters. HM and Digby were alone in the dining room enjoying a wholesome breakfast, and Peg had told them not to wait for Mr. & Mrs. Piggleford who would be down later. It was after the grapefruit segments and halfway through the eggs and bacon that Eustace appeared, looking as if a vampire had feasted on him during the night. His usual ruddy complexion was now a sickly white, his face lightly lacerated from the struggle, and his eye - now hidden under tinted glasses - bore the blueberry stain left by Sheila's fist. HM and Digby had diplomatically retired to their rooms the previous evening while Eustace was busy mollifying his overwrought and over emotional wife, but Eustace wasn't sure how much of Sheila's bizarre behaviour his guests may have witnessed.

'I trust you slept well, gentlemen?' he strained to ask, and they both enthusiastically replied they had. 'Sheila says to apologise about last night. Silly woman was looking for a lost earring or something, and slipped into the pool. I tried to catch her, grazed my damn face in the process,' he said with a feeble laugh, as he cautiously prodded his cheekbone. 'However, all's well and she's taking a light breakfast in bed this morning, I hope you'll excuse her absence.'

'Oh, of course, of course. It was a most enjoyable evening and an excellent meal,' HM said, without a trace of insincerity in his voice, and Digby could only wonder if HM had, perhaps, genuinely enjoyed the meal.

The drive back to Happy Hog Farm was tormentingly uncomfortable, as Eustace Piggleford's Range Rover bumped through rutted tracks, with screen wipers battling slashing rain and splats of mud. The radio's powerful volume discharged the news and weather while Eustace shouted above it, describing the art of pie technology and trumpeting the virtues of his factory manager, while puffing on another foul smelling pipe. As the vehicle approached the entrance to Happy Hog Farm, the sinister one-dimensional rain-soaked pig, brandishing its cleaver and pan, seemed to be crying tears of joy at their return, and Digby looked away, certain he'd seen a tongue flick out from under the dripping piggy snout.

Sublime relief it was when they arrived inside the yard and were hurriedly ushered into the second Portakabin away from the pounding downpour.

'Here he is!' said Eustace as he introduced his guests to Oswald Pike. 'This is the man that makes it all work, he's the gaffer.' Oswald Pike puffed out his chest like some strutting cock sparrow.

'Fell off yer bike then?' the spotty-faced general manager commented on observing Eustace's abused face.

'Just a little accident,' Eustace curtly responded.

Oswald cackled and a few strips of his centre-parted greased-back ginger hair sprang out of place and wavered over his forehead like broad blades of terra-cotta grass. His inane grin revealed a set of crooked protruding teeth, which clearly didn't enjoy the attention of a toothbrush very regularly. But it was Oswald's fingers which Digby noted with truly alarming disbelief. The un-manicured nails were packed with black grease. A steady chattering issued from an ancient coffee making device on top of Oswald's filing cabinet, and the sound rapidly rose to a dangerous whistle as sepia coloured liquid spurted into a well stained glass jug, pervading the office with a strange aroma.

'Wha hey, there she goes!' Oswald uttered, his high-pitched grating accent sounding like a boy with a permanently breaking voice. 'Coffee, gents?' he squeaked, and they sat themselves onto a selection of loose-jointed chairs while Oswald called to the open door. 'Rowena!' he croaked, losing command of his pitch and a petite, pale, ill-looking young girl teetered into their company on clumpy platform shoes. The bleached and spike-haired Rowena continually sniffed through a small upturned red, piggy, studded nose, and with an expression of wide-eyed incomprehension on seeing the visitors, set down a tray containing an assortment of cracked mugs still wet from the cursory rinse they had been blessed with. HM's mug bore the legend, *you can bite my sausage anytime,* beneath a picture of the prancing pig, and he examined this rare work of pottery-craft with an amused chuckle.

'That's a little promotional gimmick I did fer the local agricultural show last year,' Oswald sniggered through plaque-coated teeth, as the permanently bewildered Rowena offered a cracked bowl of sugar.

Outside the rain had abated and the four men walked towards the production buildings. Eustace excused himself and broke away to his

The Besting of Humphrey Mercer

office, leaving HM and Digby to endure their educational tour in the capable charge of this grinning, gangly man, with grease stains on the lapels and cuffs of his, at one time, white coat.

'We'll start with the smoke house, go through the production line and finish in packing,' Oswald informed his visitors, as they ambled towards a redbrick building. The smoke house door shrieked on its hinges as Oswald pulled at the handle to reveal a gloomy dark void. As daylight seeped into the Stygian haze, a vast cavern lined with thick layers of shiny black tar became visible, and bituminous stalactites hung from the ceiling causing HM to exhale a quiet whistle.

'What causes all this then?' he asked.

'Smoking, bloody years and years of smoking bacon, an' we use sawdust as the smoking material.'

'Oak or apple?' Digby knowledgeably enquired.

'No, well yes, both! Whatever we can get really; why we can even burn old socks in there,' and Oswald's high cackle pierced the warm moist air like the intermittent stuttering of a machine gun.

The trip through the butchery room would have caused iron men to faint and Digby gasped at the sickly ripe aroma arising as two barbarians in blood-stained aprons hacked and sawed various animal carcasses, filling large square metal containers with unappetising viscera. The inedible contents included ears, tubes, lungs, bones, gristle and anything that could be reclaimed from the crates of pig waste stacked around them. A large Frankenstein creation, clad in a yellow plastic overall with matching rubber boots and wearing a white forage cap with the pig logo embroidered on it, gloomily fed this putrid biological hash into a hopper at the top of a whirring pulverising machine, while Del Shannon's falsetto issuing from the tannoy rendered "Runaway" above the giant mincer's din. The mincer's minder inter-fed the hopper with handfuls of powdered rusk, copious shakings of salt, blocks of lard, pink dye and measures of preservative, while Oswald attempted a light-hearted commentary above the charivari of this charnel house. The correct amount of additives was judged by the slow man's instinct rather than by accurate measurement, making the whole process a very casual affair. A juddering larval flow of pink slime issued from a spout at the side of the "Titan mighty mincer made in Edgebaston". This, Oswald proclaimed, was your actual pie and sausage meat.

'So there you are, nothing goes to waste in here, waste not want not, eh?' Oswald's rasping laugh merged with the machine's crunching and ripping melody as the blubbery mix was collected into plastic containers and conveyed to the sausage making room.

The sausage room rang with the laughter of several fat, jolly ladies with pork sausage fingers. Sitting at their sausage machines, the unsavoury mix - courtesy of Edgbaston's mighty mincer - was forced like pink toothpaste from a long nozzle by means of a foot pedal, into an endless thin-skin tube, described as "processed edible membrane". The happy ladies skilfully twisted and turned the pink extrusion, knotting it into regular lengths and snipping off skeins of plump uncooked bangers, which were then hung on steel hooks to await the packers' attentions. Oswald approached one of the ladies with her hair pushed into what resembled a shower cap.

'Woss that remind you of then?' he squeezed a fat sausage with his forefinger and thumb. 'Bet your ol' man ain't seen 'is fer years.' The plump ladies rocked and cackled with such volume that HM and Digby covered their ears while the tannoy now offered Peter Sellers singing "Bangers and Mash". Oswald turned to his guests and winked. 'You'd be amazed at what goes into the Great British Banger!'

'I don't think we will be any more,' Digby wryly added, and Oswald burst into another round of staccato laughter.

The pastry room was a further revelation.

Six young girls in white coats and white hats were dusting white flour over small pre-formed pastry lids, which were then glued onto cups of uncooked short crust filled with pink slime. Enveloped in a fine mist, their eyes were little more than black holes blinking from white round faces, giving them the appearance of characters from a Chinese theatre. They giggled in their industry frequently dropping pastry onto the floor. The tannoy now crooned "A Whiter Shade of Pale", and Digby could contain himself no longer.

'Where on earth does this crazy music come from?' he asked.

Oswald quizzically cocked his head to one side. 'Well, from them speakers of course.' He pointed a grimy spatulate finger to the dust-laden, thick cobwebbed, steel-girdered roof. Digby burst into laughter.

'No, I mean where did you obtain such an extraordinary selection of old tunes? Even I can remember some of these.'

'Oh,' Oswald let go a short burst of cackling, 'thass 'imself, the boss, 'ees got a big collection of old vinyls what 'ee puts onto them disc things for us wiv 'is computer. Keeps us all ennertained like don't it?'

The Besting of Humphrey Mercer

A wave of hot air engulfed the visitors as they entered the bakery, where a large sweating baker heaved trays of pies from the mouth of a rumbling, hissing baking machine. The freshly cooked fare was stacked onto wheeled racks, ready for the packing unit. On passing the tall square stacks of hot steaming pork pies, Oswald caught HM absent-mindedly staring open-mouthed at one of the racks. Misinterpreting HM's expression for hunger, he plucked up a fresh pie from a tray, broke it in two and plunged one half into HM's mouth.

'Go on! I can see you're dying to try one.' Digby was at great pains to prevent himself from choking with laughter as HM stood shocked rigid with hot pie wedged into his face. But Digby's schadenfreude was short lived. Oswald then pressed the other greasy half into Digby's mouth. 'And you!' he followed.

Back out in the yard, the unpredictable climate had provided brilliant dazzling sunshine, which temporarily blinded the three men as they emerged from the building. The door closed on "Donald Wha's Ya Trewsers", and Digby inconspicuously removed his portion of pie from his mouth and dropped it into a nearby waste bin.

Everything damp had begun to evaporate in steady wisps of white vapour, and a tractor could be heard slowly chugging towards the yard from the main gate.

'Whah ho!' Oswald yelled, 'here comes the next batch of Kievs!' The tractor ground past towing a trailer piled high with wire crates packed with sad old hens, some dead, many barely alive, and all devoid of most of their feathers, which had been rubbed away or pecked out due to the cruelly crowded conditions in which they had been kept. They patiently awaited their fate, clucking and pecking in the sun's blaze. Digby's alarmed expression prompted another gem from Oswald's sad repertoire of witty comments.

'Them buggers won't need much pluckin', will they?' He turned in the direction of the tractor and shouted, 'I said, them bugger's don't need much pluckin', do they?' Cackling, he walked over to the parked vehicle and exchanged a few hearty words with the driver, before hurriedly returning to where HM and Digby stood.

'So where do you keep the pigs?' Digby asked Oswald. 'It's called Happy Hog Farm.'

'We don't keep any pigs here, 'aven't done fer years; we get all the pig stuff we need from the local abattoir, much cheaper. Come on let's away fer lunch.'

The sun shone hard as the three men walked towards the main gate, where Eustace was waiting with the Range Rover. White light bathed the yard, and a man silhouetted by the glare pushed a high trolley stacked with pies to the packing department. He gaped at the two smart men from London, who were doubtless off to enjoy an expensive lunch with the boss.

'So! What d'you think of it so far?' Eustace asked with a proud grin as the visitors approached him. "Rubbish" was in Digby's mind but both he and HM nodded in unison each hoping the other would say something intelligent about their recent experience.

It was to be Digby who adroitly responded. 'Well, I have to say, Eustace, er, that WE are most impressed.' Digby used the Royal WE as all good advertising people do, especially when not wishing to commit themselves personally to an opinion. 'WE had no idea of what goes on inside a modern food factory, and Oswald has been a most enlightening guide, hasn't he Humphrey?'

HM could still taste the uninvited pork pie and merely nodded.

'I think these gennelmen must be starvin' by now after seeing all that food,' Oswald enthusiastically commented.

'Looks like *he's* been into it already,' Eustace said, noticing the crumbs and flour smeared around HM's mouth. 'Right let's away then - you drive Oswald - we'll go to Clarence's, I think.' Eustace handed a wildly grinning Oswald the car keys, while HM and Digby climbed into the back of the Range Rover.

During the rough ride which followed, Eustace talked obsessively about quotas and wastage, while occasionally glancing over his shoulder to repeat a statistic or two for the advertising men's benefit. Digby set his mind into speculation about the cuisine at Clarence's; the name had an air of class about it. He was quite looking forward to perusing the menu; assuming he could still eat after having endured Oswald's driving. Clearly Oswald was not in full harmony with the car's efficient breaking system judging by the number of times HM and Digby came close to sharing the front seat with him, only to be forced violently back again by a sudden stamp on the gas pedal. Mercifully the ride came to a sudden stop in front of "The Halfway House", a small, uninteresting pub, seemingly in the middle of nowhere.

'Come on, gentlemen, stretch your legs,' Eustace called, as he climbed out of the car. He walked to the rear hatch, with Oswald hopping after him like an expectant child outside a sweet shop.

The Besting of Humphrey Mercer

'Must be stopping for a quick beer then, great!' HM said cheerfully, as he and Digby clambered from the high cabin. After a few moments of rummaging at the back of the car, Oswald re-appeared carrying a deep plastic container packed with Piggleford's pies and sausages.

'In we go then!' Eustace exhorted, as he locked the car. The four men entered a dimly lit bar with a cold brick floor, and all conversation ceased. A straggle of gaping zombies at the far end of the room stared as the visitors walked towards the counter, and their eyes scanned every movement of HM and Digby as the two well-dressed men stood at the bar beside Eustace.

'Your nephew's brought you the pies and sausages you ordered,' Eustace called out to a large man shadowed behind the bar, as Oswald slammed the heavily loaded container onto the counter. The zombies remained silent, but two poacher vagabonds standing away from the others were sly-spying HM and Digby with amused interest.

'Mornin', Mr. Piggleford, hor, looks like you've bin in a bit ov' a foight with the missus,' said the landlord as he materialised into the light. 'Mornin', Ozzie lad, alright then?' The landlord was a large bullock of a man with close-set squinting eyes which didn't appear to look directly at whomever he was addressing. He had the same stained tombstone teeth of his nephew Oswald. Wire wool sideburns vigorously bloomed from either side of his wide squat head.

'We've got two guests from Lunnon for lunch. Think you can fill 'em up?' Oswald announced by way of introduction. The Cheshire cat grinning host extended a warm large chubby hand across the bar to HM and Digby.

'Pleased t' meet yer, gennelmen, Clarence Pike's the name!' HM and Digby took it in turns to have their hands powerfully crushed by this huge ham-armed, avuncular old salt. Wincing they uttered their names and a deep, gloom of disappointment enveloped Digby as he realised that this pub was *Clarence's*, the restaurant at which they were to eat lunch. The zombies' conversation whisperingly resumed and the two poacher pirates conjectured on how they could relieve the two London pansies of their over-privileged wealth. Their barely legal rust bucket of a van in the pub car park, hoarded an assortment of illegally acquired pigeons, pheasants and rabbits, to offload onto any potential customer they could ensnare.

'That's no problem now Oswald's brought us the supplies,' Clarence boomed, 'I'll see what the ol' trout in the kitchen's up to!'

As the huge man disappeared with Piggleford's produce, Digby became concerned by Oswald's behaviour. He was doubled over painfully, attempting to suppress a neighing sound in response to Clarence's rustic quip, hissing and choking in the process.

'Thass my aunt - 'ee calls 'er the ole trout!' he guffawed. Clarence reappeared rubbing his lardy hands around an ample girth.

'Daisy sends 'er regards Mr. Piggleford, She'll be out in a moment t' say hallo. In the meantime, can I get you some drinks, gennelmen?'

HM stepped forward reaching into his inside pocket, and the larger of the two poachers nudged the other. The latter leered salaciously with blackened stumps of teeth, in anticipation of sighting HM's over-burdened wallet.

'No, no, I'll get these,' Eustace insisted. 'You can pay for the food alright?'

Beers pulled, they all steered themselves to an alcove at the opposite end of the bar from the zombies. Once settled, a large moon-faced woman silently appeared in front of them holding a notepad and pencil. Oswald jumped up.

'Allo, Aunt Daisy,' he gave her a peck on the cheek, 'these gennelmen are advertising executives from Lunnon.' She dipped and shyly smiled her head oscillating from side to side.

'Mornin', gentlemen, and mornin', Mr. Piggleford.'

Daisy was an affable person, stoutly built like her husband with a smudge of fine dark hair along her upper lip. She was simply dressed in a thin floral cotton dress and brown cardigan and stood in scuffed pink trainers with no laces, her swollen ankles having necessitated their removal.

'These chaps have come all the way from London to sample your legendary fare,' Eustace said, 'so what can y' do for us?'

Daisy blushed and laughed a little at the compliment, before proceeding to articulate as clearly as possible the legendary bill of fare. 'Wal, oi can do sossidge toad, chips an' peas, 'ot or cold pork pie or chicken an 'am pie with chips an' peas, Spanish or cheese omlitt with chips an' peas, or I've got....' she stopped.

Oswald was inanely grinning and rubbing his hands vigorously together as he fidgeted on his chair like an excited monkey. 'Go on, say it,' he squawked bobbing his head up and down. Digby wondered what quintessence of culinary witchcraft could be causing so much simian excitement in Mr Oswald Pike. Daisy confidently resumed her run-down of the day's menu.

'Wal oi've got a new dish today,' Daisy said. Oswald gurgled like a mewling child and rapidly and drummed his clenched fist up and down on his knee as she announced, 'Chopped Chicken Kiev!'

The Besting of Humphrey Mercer

'You've gotta have it!' Oswald wailed to Digby and HM, 'an' with all the trimmins.'

'Oh! no, really we couldn't. It's very nice of you but we had Piggleford's Chicken Kiev last night, and delicious it was too,' HM insisted. Digby was astounded by HM's easy hypocrisy.

The larger pirate stroked the iron filings on his chin, cracking his mouth into a wide predatory grin.

'But *this* is Piggleford's too!' Oswald enthused. 'All the pies, sausages and stuff here is ours. Come on go fer it!'

'Now let them decide for themselves,' Eustace butted in to Digby's relief, 'we all had it last night, so we'll have something different. You have the Chopped Chicken Kiev, Oswald.' He smiled and winked at Oswald. 'Bet you could eat two of them.'

Digby chose an omelette in the belief that only a complete culinary incompetent could ruin a cheese omelette, and if he was condemned to eat rubbish it could at least be washed down with the not unpleasant beer Clarence kept.

The two poacher pirates drained their glasses and rose from where they had been watching the two London pansies. As they left, the larger pirate turned back to the counter and shouted to Clarence Pike. 'Cheers, Clari, we're off to the Ferrets now!' and, with a wink, spoke loudly in Digby's direction. 'They're doing poached salmon 'an pigeon casserole today!' Digby who had just taken a good draught of his beer choked violently, spraying the table with good ale.

'Ass orroight, now garn with yer, fack orf!' Clarence playfully scolded as he put two fingers up at the departing rapscallions.

Back at Happy Hog farm, Digby kept a keen eye on his wristwatch, willing the hands to move faster. They were at the end of their tour and would soon be collected by taxi to catch the train back to London. The last item on the agenda was a visit to the laboratory and a meeting with Suresh Vakram, a meeting which Eustace had dismissed as of no real interest, but as they had to wait for their cab, Digby politely insisted on a quick visit. HM and he were left alone with Suresh Vakram, the highly qualified doctor of chemistry, the man whom Eustace impertinently referred to as Harry Krishna.

The white-coated biochemist was a slightly built man. His deep brown Indian eyes were dark-ringed through lack of sleep, and his mien was of one with the troubles of the world upon his shoulders. He sat among test tubes, clamps and beakers, sighing over the inconsistent quantities of additives and fat, which regularly appeared in Piggleford's products. He shook his head at certain questions put to him. He was not a happy man and looked extremely relieved when the oscillating smiling face of Eustace's secretary Debsie appeared at the little window of the laboratory door to summon his two visitors.

'Your taxi will be arriving soon,' Debsie said, and Suresh smiled with great relief. He grabbed his coat, and muttering an apology, left the office like someone late for a train. Digby was puzzled; there was something familiar about Debsie's odd visage, and a thought formed in the far recesses of his memory, as she closed the laboratory door and led them back to Eustace's office.

'We had lunch at the halfway house today,' Digby said to her. 'Do you know it?'

'Know it!' Debsie smiled, pushing her ample chest towards him. 'Should do: it's my parent's place'.

The taxi eventually arrived and Eustace gave Digby and Rod a hearty handshake, while Oswald stood ceremoniously holding the car's door open.

'Er, I hope Mr Vakram was suitably favourable in his opinion of our product?' he quietly said to Digby.

'Oh gracious, couldn't have been more enthusiastic!' Digby so easily fibbed.

'Excellent! Well, good to have met you both, and I'll expect to see some clever packaging ideas from your creative genii in a couple weeks or so, eh?' Eustace said, 'Sheila phoned earlier to say good-bye. She's sorry she couldn't be here to see you, but she's had to go to see her sister in London who's not too well.'

'Oh, I am sorry,' HM answered. 'Thank you for your marvellous hospitality, and tell Sheila that whenever she's in London again to look us up at the agency. We'd be glad to see her anytime.' Digby shuddered at the thought and wondered how HM could appear to be so enthusiastic over a prospect he himself would deplore, but it was a fair bet that she would do no such thing anyway, he reasoned.

The train journey back to London was sheer heaven for HM and Digby. They were comfortably seated in a first class compartment with two large gin and tonics. The view across the wide countryside was bliss compared with the visit they had left behind them. The brilliant rose-carmine blaze of the falling sun projected dark tree shadows across fields where still sheep glowed like little cream coloured farmyard toys on

The Besting of Humphrey Mercer

sage baize. Ruminating cows flicked their tails, and in the distance a chestnut mare galloped along a fence as if racing the train.

This was peace indeed and the two travellers nodded into a delicious sleep.

When HM and Digby's train arrived at London, the evening sky was already graduating to purple. They joined the long line of impatient and travel-weary passengers waiting for taxis and were exchanging memories of the funnier aspects of their trip, when HM took a sharp in-take of breath.' Look! Up ahead, Digby. Isn't that Sheila Piggleford?' he whispered.

Digby craned his neck to see through the forest of swaying and bobbing heads before him. 'Well I'm blessed, so it is,' Digby confirmed stroking his chin. 'I didn't see her at the other end, did you?'

'No, perhaps she got on at a different station. Wonder what she's up to.'

They watched unseen as Sheila climbed into a cab with a familiar looking man. That man was Suresh Vakram. The door slammed, and the taxi disappeared into the London traffic.

Malcolm was a sad dreamer

Chapter 7   Mr M.C.P.

Malcolm Campbell Patterson examined his tired face in the mirror. It was 6.30 a.m. and the rest of Malcolm's house was still in slumber. Small beads of moisture erupted along his forehead and top lip, which he hoped were the result of the recent hot shower he had taken. Sadly, they were the manifestation of injudicious boozing. Malcolm had demolished the larger half of a bottle of whisky the previous evening after his wife and two young children had gone to bed.

Despite having been denied the opportunity to follow-up the Piggleford's business, Malcolm could, at last, prove himself a worthy and successful advertising entrepreneur, for on this morning following HM's return from Piggleford's, he was preparing to prove his worth with a stunning new business coup.

Although Malcolm had fallen demonstrably short of his projected claim of thirty per cent increase in company turnover in the next year, he was now on the brink of a venture which would secure for him the most ingratiating of respect. He fantasised that women in the office would swoon in adoration as he walked by; HM would be entreating him to accept a 20% stake in the company as a gift of appreciation; that

The Besting of Humphrey Mercer

French tart Susanne Vérdier, who'd engineered his alcoholic humiliation in the wine bar; would be ordered to scrub out the office urinals every morning with her bare hands; and the fat arsed Angela Bottomly would be forced on her knees to publicly lick his shoes clean everyday, after he'd first ground them in dogshit of course.

Malcolm Campbell Patterson was a sad and twisted dreamer. He was a depressing example of someone who'd never learned to control his lust for opportunity, nor to recognise the vipers who made up the real world of hustlers and conmen. Malcolm was bedazzled by the advertising world - while possessing scant knowledge of its complexities - and despite having failed in his past ventures as a salesperson, believed advertising to be his true calling. He was poorly equipped to cope with the politically driven treachery that so often festers beneath the thick skin of this profession's perceived air of glamour and excitement.

In short, Malcolm was the classic stooge.

He stuck out like a hooker at a Sunday school picnic and had that come help yourself to my expense account look, written all over him. Indeed many a dodgy brand manager, publicity director or marketing manager took advantage of him by dangling the carrot of a big business deal before his eager little ego. These seasoned freeloaders would wreak havoc with Malcolm's wallet, leaching as many long lunches, football and theatre tickets as his credit cards would yield. What he gained by way of business in return wouldn't have paid for his parking fines, but sadly, the request for a simple T-shirt design would move Malcolm to leaping and punching the air in jubilation, convinced that he was on the brink of winning a lucrative contract.

But today was a new start as far as he was concerned. Today was the big one. This was the coup, which would confound and silence his detractors.

Malcolm was to attend an early morning breakfast meeting at the Savoy Hotel in London with his new business contact - a prospect HM had not been convinced about after having been eagerly informed by Malcolm of this *dead cert* opportunity. "He was in front of so much business he didn't know which way to turn". This was a phrase Malcolm used frequently in an attempt to rally the support of his colleagues. For many months he had been drawing a salary, had been claiming expenses and had had the use of a new company car in his role as "new business whizz kid". The only whizzing he had done to date was through the company chequebook, a waggish accounts clerk had remarked.

During his job interview with HM, Malcolm had imprudently declared that several large companies were very keen to place their business with him, should he find a suitably professional advertising agency to back him, and he quoted some very impressive names. HM had been foolish enough to believe these wild claims, eschewing all advice to the contrary from his colleagues; Malcolm did not enjoy the most flattering of reputations among those who knew him from the past, and whisperings of his incompetence circulated freely and without hindrance in the pubs and bars frequented by print reps., and other sundry bag carriers and sales people.

Ironically, it was HM's inability to admit his mistake in hiring Malcolm, which accounted for his relatively long rate of survival at M&AD. Malcolm for his part did arrive at the office early each morning, which gratified HM no end, and rarely left before 7.30 p.m., especially if the hospitality room drinks cabinet was open. But it was Malcolm's schedule during the working day that gave rise to much speculation. Each morning at around 11.00 a.m. he would emerge from his office where he had been busy checking his emails and making important telephone calls, to move his car to another parking meter. He would depart looking a little shaky to return at around noon, perky as a parrot. "Le Cochonne" - as this baby-faced, baggy-suited plump man with thinning fair hair and a Pekingese nose had been labelled by Susanne Vérdier - would then casually wander into various offices, enquiring with a ventriloquist's squawk, 'Are we winning then?' followed by the predictable cry, 'I'm in front of so much business I don't know which way to turn.' The pungent whiff of whisky on his breath escaped no one. At 1.00 p.m., unless lunching with someone in the office, he would disappear for most of the afternoon leaving the anxious receptionist with the unenviable task of inventing plausible excuses for his absence, a skill in which he kept her motivated with regular bribes of cheap perfume and chocolate - purchased from his expense account - which this underpaid and much put-upon lonely lady treasured.

Malcolm's drive into London was as uneventful as it always was. If there had been a road accident, or if a high-speed police car chase had passed him, it is doubtful that he would have noticed anything unusual. Malcolm stared hard ahead, un-blinking, while his car purred forward seemingly without any instruction from its driver. He manipulated the controls in a smiling trance, little more than a robot making pre-programmed

The Besting of Humphrey Mercer

movements, which appeared to require no effort or thought on his part. His thoughts were far away in another land, and in another time.

Malcolm had first encountered Allen J. Humbucker at the end of a fruitless business trip during a previous short-lived employment, selling silk-screen printing services to the USA. On the final evening of this venture, he was in a bar sipping expense account whisky and killing an hour or so before heading to the airport for his flight home. The only other person in the bar was a tall man sitting opposite, who was watching him with predatory intent. Hunched over his drink, unaware of his observer, and depressed at the prospect of returning home with nothing to show for his travels, Malcolm was suddenly presented with a last glimmer of hope.

Many Americans will readily make conversation with a complete stranger and Allen J. Humbucker was no exception.

'You English?' he shouted across the bar. Malcolm quickly straightened his back and quietly replied that he certainly was.

'Jeez, ah just cain't git over that crazy accent you guys have,' Allen J - as he would have Malcolm address him in future - chuckled. He directed his loud voice to the other end of the counter. 'Hey, bartender! Git this man another of whatever it is he's drinking!' It wasn't long before Allen J moved around the horseshoe shaped mahogany counter to where Malcolm was sitting. Names were exchanged, hands vigorously shaken, professions revealed and business cards swapped.

Allen J was in cardboard. His belt was made from cardboard. 'Look at that!' he yelled, with thumbs thrust down behind his waistband. 'Pure kurdboard! Looks like hide, don't it?' His suit, needless to say, was made from real material. 'Ponderosa Pulp Inc. reclaims millions of tons of supermarket kurdboard waste every year!' Allen J declaimed to a starry-eyed Malcolm Campbell Patterson, 'an we process it t' make useful merchandise.' Malcolm nodded, suitably impressed. 'Whah, even mah shoes are kurdboard. An' this!' Allen J fumbled into his briefcase and thrust an object at a hesitant Malcolm. 'Take it!' Malcolm gingerly received the strange item, and turned it around in his hand feigning intense study. It took the form of two light brown, highly polished wings, chrome hinged at the centre, with a set of stiff black bristles at either end, reminiscent of epaulettes, a sort of folding brush he conjectured. 'You're durn right! It's a collapsible clothes brush an' coat hanger, an' it's all made from one hundred percent k-u-r-d-board, 'cept the bristles of course,' Allen J triumphantly declared.

'All very green and ecologically sound,' Malcolm enthused.

'Green, my ass! To hell with all that ecology shit, This is business man, b-i-g bucks; that's what it's all about, an' it's all here in kurdboard!' Allen J commanded, stabbing a long forefinger at the item Malcolm held. His voice suddenly dropped to a near whisper, as he leaned forward, fixing Malcolm with his slate grey eyes. 'And ah'm lookin' fur people who's got the appetite fur opportunity.' Allen J screwed a wink at Malcolm, as he drew back with a chuckle, snatched up his drink and drained it. 'Yes, sir, the same again please!' he bellowed to the barman. Malcolm was feeling a little giddy, and the combination of alcohol, along with the thrilling expectation of becoming involved in a big business deal, filled him with a very pleasant floating sensation. 'Pity you've gotta be leaving tonight, Malcolm,' Allen J said, in mock concern, slyly spying him from behind his raised glass. 'You could be just the kinda guy ah need.' The carefree euphoria, which had taken command of Malcolm's will power, convinced him not to miss out on a sure-fire business opportunity, and thoughts of cancelling his return flight to stay over one more night immediately sprung into his mind. Yes, he'd even take Allen J to dinner. At Malcolm's hesitant proposal to this effect Allen J became adamantly assertive.

'No, you will not, sir! You're a guest in mah country, an' ah'm takin' you to dinner, an' if you like good meat ah know a place where they do great Cajun beef 'n black butter.'

'Well perhaps you'll let me pay for the drinks then?'

'That you most certainly can do, sir,' Allen J promptly replied.

Allen J Humbucker was a tall and well-preserved man. He owned a head of thick steel grey hair, which crowned a bronzed, weathered face and radiated a fitness, which belied his 67 years. He eulogised with much authority on the merits of good Scotch whisky and wines, and spoke with almost childish enthusiasm about the various culinary skills he and his wife Beulah possessed - or Boo-boo, as he endearingly termed her. Allen J proudly made much of his specious British origins, declaring that more than a hint of Scottish blood coursed through his veins. Humbucker didn't sound very Gaelic to Malcolm's mind, but he declined to comment.

The very expensive restaurant Allen J had recommended very conveniently didn't accept Allen J's brand of credit card, so Malcolm was saddled with the food bill also. By then he really didn't care, nor did he care about the cost of the many bottles of fine vintage wine and the generous quantity of cognac his host had ordered. Allen J resolved to pay

The Besting of Humphrey Mercer

Malcolm back thirty fold on his soon-to-be trip to England, when the two of them would talk "real business".

And that was the last Malcolm heard of Allen J. Humbucker for two years.

Dismissed from Ay Bee Cee ScreenPrint, on his return to England, Malcolm wrote letters to which Allen J never responded. He neither returned any telephone messages or emails from Malcolm, who sadly hoped that the elusive American would one day fulfil his obligation. Surprise it was then, when Malcolm received a letter at his home address demanding a breakfast meeting at the Savoy Hotel, with Allen J, Humbucker to discuss BIG BUSINESS. Now he could support his previous claims and prove his worth to HM.

Malcolm blinked out of his reverie as his car slid along Charing Cross embankment. He parked at the Savoy's back entrance, smiled at his image in the rear view mirror as he adjusted his tie, and crossed his fingers before easing himself out of the company saloon.

'Hi, Malcolm, ol' buddy, how y' doing there?' Grinning and over effusive as ever, Allen J. Humbucker rose from the breakfast table and grasped Malcolm's hand, causing him to wince at the powerful grip. 'This is mah wife Beaulah. Boo-boo, this here's Malcolm ah been tellin' y' all about.' A tall willowy, swan-necked woman in her late 50's offered a slender bejewelled hand and smiled with huge white teeth, which accentuated her long equine face. Her movement was slow and almost graceful.

'Pleased t' meet you,' Beaulah intoned in a similar, softer, and more nasal dialect than her husband's. Malcolm nodded and smiled. He was shaking a little as he took her hand and a rash of perspiration broke across his forehead and top lip again. When they were all sitting, Allen J ordered breakfast. Beaulah poured tea while the two men exchanged pleasantries and recounted memories of their first meeting.

'So how's the pulp business?' Malcolm asked the president of Ponderosa Pulp Inc. Allen J was stuffing a croissant into his mouth and answered while chewing.

'Not in it anymore, got out!' He chewed some more and took a swig of tea. 'No way hose-ay!' He wiped his mouth with a Savoy embroidered linen napkin. 'Personal attack products, that's the future.' He took another gulp of tea. 'B-i-g business I tell you, what with all this friggin' violence goin' on ever' where!' Boo-boo nodded, pulling her gaunt face into an expression of disdain. 'People need protection, an' they'll pay well for it!' Allen J slid into a badly attempted English accent. 'Now this is where you come in, Mr Campbell Patterson, old boy!' Boo-boo covered her mouth as she released a delicate giggle, and Malcolm heroically managed a contrived chuckle. Allen J returned to his native dialect. 'Ah want you to git some product movin' for me in the UK, get t' gether a good team an' clean up! Told y' ah'd pay y' back.'

Malcolm gulped his tea, trying hard not to appear too eager, now desperate for success. 'What sort of products are they?' he quickly enquired.

'Miniature shriekers, CS gas dispensers, personal attack alarms, you name it we can securitise it! Take your average briefcase fur starters: we can fit it with a handle so as when y' squeeze it hurd, it sets off a shrieker that can be heard near on two mile away; would jus' deafen any would-be mugger; an' if that don't stop the fucker, why it'll shoot out gas into his face as well!'

'Allen Jay, please,' Boo-boo interjected, with exaggerated concern, 'remember where y' are.' Allen J's voice dropped instantly.

'Sorry, Boo.' He turned to Malcolm. 'Now here's the best part, we can make gas-discharging handles t' fit walking sticks fur the old folks, fur suitcases, fur brollies, an' we even got a shrieking gasser that can fit in a snapshot or video camera fur people on their holidays. We've got a purse gasser fur the ladies, an' this,' he took a fat looking fountain pen from his breast pocket and aimed it at Malcolm's face, 'this'll shoot stuff in your eyes that'll blind you fur near on haf' 'n hour.' Malcolm instinctively drew back from the pen. 'It's OK, it's perfectly hurmless, jus' stings yer eyes out fur a bit, that's all,' Allen J assured him.

Malcolm was trying hard to enter into the spirit of Mr Humbucker's enthusiasm, but wasn't sure how to tackle this one; he desperately needed to consult Digby Hope, or even HM.

'Well Allen J, I must say that this all sounds very interesting, and I'd very much like you to meet a couple of my colleagues for their input so that we can discuss this further,' he said, a little nervously. Allen J sat back in wide-eyed surprise.

'Discuss further! Huh, what's there to discuss further?'

'Well, I'd just like you to meet the MD of my new company and our marketing expert. They will undoubtedly have, er, some useful views on how to approach the UK market and make sure that the, er, law would allow such devices in a public place, that sort of thing,' Malcolm was

The Besting of Humphrey Mercer

beginning to fumble for reasons, and Allen J began to regard him with suspicion.

'In mah book crime's crime, an' the law's there to be obeyed in whatever country an' in whatever language! People have got a right to protection from Bastards who break the law!'

'Allen Jay, please! You know ah don't like to hear such language,' Beaulah instantly shrieked. Allen J had become over emotional; he calmed down and apologised at his wife's stern insistence.

'OK! OK! ah'm sorry. So let's meet your guys if you think it's gonna help. Ah'm willin' t' hear what they've got t' say, an' what investment they're prepared t' make. But Malc,' he suddenly gripped Malcolm's forearm, 'you're my main man, right?'

'Er, well, yes, yes of course,' Malcolm assured him, alarmed by the unexpected power of this aggressive gesture, 'I'll set up a meeting for tomorrow if that's convenient.' Malcolm was assured it was.

HM was visibly intimidated by the tall American when they met the following day. The conference room table bore some samples of the agency's work, casually scattered across it. A flip chart and easel stood carelessly in the corner on unequally extended legs. Digby sauntered into the room with a singularly unimpressed air. He'd shown not a jot of interest in personal attack products. He droned a brief, uninspired overview of the agency's credentials before offering his own opinion of Allen J's business, moribundly lecturing about product proposition, creative strategy and market research. Allen J was beginning to frown, while Malcolm marvelled, not comprehending a word of Digby's rhetorical eloquence, but was highly impressed for all that.

HM spoke next. He rose from the table, snapped his back straight and strutted to and fro' while sputtering about the importance of safety and the legal implications pertaining to the use of gas in a public place, a concept which most decidedly appealed to him. He talked about the approximate costs to produce an advertising campaign of any weight. His manner was of one delivering a stilted sermon, as he stared at the ceiling, pinching his chin and addressing nobody in particular, least of all Allen J himself. He adopted the superior and patronising manner of one who assumed Allen J to be a naive country hick. Malcolm was as confused and out of his depth as ever, and sat silently opening and closing his mouth like some bloated goldfish, unsuccessfully trying to contribute a word or two.

Allen J's brow was furrowed with increasing irritation. He had remained quiet for long enough, he thought, as he drew in air, puffing with incredulity at all of this high flown and pretentious adspeak. His patience had expired, and interrupting HM's pompous meandering, turned to Malcolm.

'Jeez, Malc, is there a misunderstanding here? What is this dipstick talking about? I don't need advertising; this stuff'll sell itself. I need investment. I need people with the balls to put their money where their mouth is. I need aggressive UK agents who'll purchase an' distribute my merchandise through selectively recruited teams, nationwide. An' clean up!' He looked towards HM, jabbing a long finger at him. 'Sell-synergy! Know anything about sell-synergy?'

HM's eyes bulged with indignation.

'I think Mr Humbucker is alluding to the dubious practice of pyramid selling,' Digby interrupted, with a sigh of boredom in his voice, 'or networking as it is sometimes known.'

Allen J immediately railed at Digby. 'Now you listen here, Sherlock Holmes. Don't you friggin' patronise me. It's nothing to do with pyramid selling: it works on an entirely different, decent an' honest principle!' He shook his head with a smile of ironic disbelief. 'Jeez, I don't believe you guys. Whah back home I know kids of eleven an' twelve who catch on quicker 'n you. I want agents that know what they're talkin' about, not a bunch of posturing stumblebums,' he looked directly at HM, 'an' I don't need some Savile Row suited short-ass tellin' me how t' advertise. I used to be in advertising. I've been there, chum!'

Quivering with rage HM's pink face became crimson. He spoke with a rising falsetto. 'I c-can assure you, Mr Humbucker...'

'You couldn't assure me you know which end you shit from, your ass or your face!' Allen J rapidly returned.

HM's face was now an indescribable colour as he stuttered in protest. 'In in that case I, I think this meeting has gone f-far enough, we are an advertising agency and not a r-recruitment office, It's clear, despite allegedly having been in advertising, that you have not got, ah, the slightest idea, ah, of what is involved in, er, promoting a new product in a new en-environment...'

'Excuse me,' Allen J calmly interrupted, 'but you know, you speak just like a goose shits, in short spurts!' He collected up his brief case. 'An' I know which ah'd prefer t' listen to.' White and trembling, Malcolm opened the door as Allen J rose from his seat. On reaching the door, he turned back to HM and Digby. 'I eat dickheads like you fur breakfast

The Besting of Humphrey Mercer

- you're not worth a bunch 'o beans. Good-day!' As Allen J moved from the room he grabbed an ashen-faced and fainting Malcolm by the hand. He winked and whispered, 'See you soon, ol' pal.'

'I'll see you out,' Malcolm croaked, and eagerly followed Allen J along the corridor to the reception, through fear of having to face the instant wrath of his boss.

Chapter 8   Exit Mr M.C.P

HM sat down hard into his chair and stared at the open door, while drumming the table with the tips of his short blunt fingernails. He expelled a long, deep sigh and looked over to Digby, who was gazing at the floor, with his interlocked fingers pushed up under his chin.

'Campbell Patterson must be mental. Where does he find these maniacs? I don't know whether to be angry or to feel sorry for the poor sod,' HM said, with remarkable calm, after the blunt abuse he'd taken. His pumped-up pomposity had been deflated, and he sought comfort in defending Malcolm's lack of judgement as being the result of a brain malfunction rather than the result of undistilled incompetence.

'Yup, he's a problem alright,' Digby suddenly replied, as he moved to close the door Malcolm had left open. 'You've got no choice, Humphrey: you've got to straighten the guy out or tell him to go. Frankly, he's a disaster.'

HM nodded his head vigorously. 'Damn it, damn it, you're right. I'll go and see him right now!'

Malcolm could not be found anywhere. Even the near hysterical Ruth Vanderstein at reception was unable to offer any explanation when sternly grilled by HM. She'd seen him at the door exchanging goodbyes with the "American gentleman", and as far as she knew Malcolm hadn't returned to his office. A gentleman is not how HM would have described this uncouth Yank who'd abused his hospitality with childish insults, and if it were not for want of preserving the agency's immaculately professional reputation, he'd have biffed the bounder on the nose. HM wandered back to his office, pressing a fist to his mouth, deep in thought. He pushed into his room, to find Angela Bottomly lounging in one of his leather chairs, her cherry red lips expelling blue smoke rings. She smiled provocatively at his surprise on seeing her, as he scoured his memory, wondering why she was there.

'You mean we have..?'

'We have,' Angela replied softly.

'A meeting?' HM was confused. The sight of Angela aroused erotic emotions within him as she always did.

The Besting of Humphrey Mercer

'Yes,' she repeated, 'a meeting about the Pearson's project you wanted me to get involved with.'

HM's memory jumped back. 'Oh yes, yes, I'm sorry, I was temporarily sidetracked,' HM said, still frowning at the bitter memory of Allen J's visit. 'You've got some ideas then?'

'Well, yes, I have, but I've also got a bit of a problem,' Angela replied, biting her bottom lip.

'A problem?'

'Yes, well, I mean the Pearson's business is really Jery Hewitt's territory, isn't it? I mean, I'd feel a bit rotten treading on his toes, and I don't think he'd be very pleased about it.' Treading on anyone's toes, let alone those of her department head, would never spark more than an atom of concern in Angela's scheming mind, and despite her apparent simpering concern for Jery's sensitivities, HM's equally evil predilection for treachery caused him to rather doubt the honesty of her solicitude. He cared no less over the bruising of people's sensitivities than she did.

The MD of Pearson's Herbal Product's Ltd., manufacturers of herbal teas and health infusions, was considering a change to his current advertising strategy. Nothing too rash or radical, just a re-jigging of their well established advertising and packaging. Mr Pearson senior would soon visit M&AD to look over some new ideas. HM had overreacted as usual, and believing that he was about to lose this long standing client, had insisted that Angela be given full rein to "think up" some entirely new concepts with which to impress Pearson's MD. She had invested many hours in swinging HM's opinion to her favour, where new, original thinking was needed, and she was now getting her chance to score points over Jery Hewitt. Angela, acutely aware of Jery's lack of faith in her talents, was murderously bent on proving him incapable of holding down the enviable position that she herself had set her sights on.

'Do not concern yourself, I've already made it quite clear to Jery that I want *you* to take the initiative on Pearson's new advertising, after all, he's busy enough with the Piggleford's pies project,' HM stared at her, stroking his thin moustache with a salacious leer, 'so what's your idea for Pearson's then?'

'Television!'

There was a moment's silence.

'What?' HM was stunned by Angela's brevity. 'Television commercials for herbal teas and health infusions?'

'Absolutely. TV's the only way to make Pearson's a household name.'

HM clutched the back of his neck, looked up at the ceiling and inhaled deeply. 'Well, it's an interesting thought, but I doubt that old man Pearson will spend that sort of money. What will the commercial be like?'

'I've got this fabulous idea for a jingle, but I need a couple of days or so to work it out, and then I'll give you something which will knock Pearson's socks off!' Angela said, with confident authority.

HM slid his hand away from the back of his neck and rubbed his chin nodding with a pained smile. 'Alright, then go ahead,' he said, slapping his knee. 'I await further developments with baited breath.' Angela slowly rose and coyly smoothed down her hitched-up dress, which had exposed more than a hint of her fleshy thigh.

'Incidentally, if you're looking for Malcolm Campbell Patterson, why don't you try Fanny's Bar?' she said, with a cruel twist to her mouth.

Nobody, except the likes of Malcolm and occasionally HM, would use Fanny's Bar, a tacky watering hole for tired and emotional sales-reps. Fanny's Bar wallowed in the basement of Duckworth's Hotel. The proprietress - well known to the local constabulary - made a lucrative living letting out rooms for the half-day, no questions asked. HM decided not to go in search of Malcolm who would doubtless by now be very drunk.

The following day, the moment he arrived in his office, HM summoned Malcolm. Malcolm could not be found for some while and eventually appeared in HM's office at lunchtime.

'Where have you been? What have you been doing?' HM demanded. 'I'm reliably informed that you spent all yesterday in Fanny's bar, after the outrageous meeting with that Humbuckle man. I've been looking for you all morning to explain these expense claims for breakfast at the Savoy, lunch at Quaglino's and taxis, for Humbuckle and his wife presumably!'

Malcolm stood like a guilty schoolboy before HM's desk. Behind HM two tall windows flooded bright late morning light around his head and shoulders, rendering him in silhouette. Malcolm was at considerable pains to see the face of his interrogator. This unpleasant interviewing tactic was one, which HM often employed when he wished to put his visitors at a disadvantage.

'I was just outside, moving my car to another parking spot,' Malcolm explained, with anxiety in his voice. Tiny beads of moisture sparkled along his top lip and the familiar aroma of cheap whisky hung around him.

The Besting of Humphrey Mercer

'But it's twelve o-clock. What in hell's name are you playing at, Malcolm?'

'I'm just trying to get on with my job, Humphrey.' Malcolm was bobbing his head from side to side, to avoid the hard sunlight flashing around HM's shadowed face.

'Trying? Trying seems to be the operative word! You made some pretty impressive new business forecasts at the time you joined us and not one of them has materialised into anything!'

'Well, you can't expect miracles overnight, Humphrey. It takes time to hook the big fish,' Malcolm feebly answered.

'I'm not looking for miracles, or fish!' HM hissed. 'I just want to know what has happened to all of this business you're in front of. And if Allen J Humbunkum, or whatever his name is, is your idea of business, then I fear your judgement is highly questionable to say the least.'

'Well, Humphrey, if you find it necessary to question my judgement, then it's plain that my effort is not appreciated.'

'Wha-at? Good God, man, I haven't seen any effort yet!'

'All I need is time.' Malcolm writhed with unease at his fatuous line of defence - he'd been here before and instinctively knew that his days were numbered.

'Time! You've been with us for near a year now and you ask for time! How long does it take to convert the business which apparently you already had in the bag?'

'Ten and a bit,' Malcolm corrected. 'I've only been here ten and a half months.' Malcolm's clottish reply further fuelled HM's fury.

'Don't you split hairs with me. Ten months is ten months too long to be on full salary, have use of a company car and be drawing out-of-pocket expenses at the rate of two or three hundred a week. And for what? For some blithering con-man selling networking. And you then have the insufferable gall to expect me to pay for wining and dining the bastard!'

'You must realise Humphrey, getting new business is not easy; as I say, it takes time to winkle out the right contacts. I've got plenty of positive longer-term promises of business, but they've got to wait for the appropriate opportunity to move the business over to me.'

'Oh come on, when the hell were you born? These bastards'll promise the hanging gardens of Babylon for a lunch. It's a way of life to these shabby freeloaders, conning gullible saps like you!'

'I object to that remark, Humphrey. I'm not exactly overpaid for what I do!' Malcolm unwisely asserted.

HM exploded. 'Overpaid!' He shot a sheet of columned figures across the desk. 'This is what you've cost the company so far in salary and expenses.' Malcolm gulped on seeing the bottom line. 'We've designed and printed three thousand T-shirts for "Fearless Freighting Services", one of your *dead cert* contacts, for which we've never been paid. You forecast at the last board meeting that they would be spending in the region of a quarter of a million pounds in advertising with us, and I've just received this letter from the liquidators telling me they've gone bust!' He threw the letter in front of Malcolm. 'I've been insulted by a homicidal maniac who wants to gas half of Britain, and you tell *me* it's not easy!' HM rose from his large leather armchair to pace the office while Malcolm sat white and shaking. 'Frankly, it'd be a damn sight better for all of us if you resigned!'

'Alright, alright, I'll resign, but it's unfair, it's unfair.' Malcolm was shaking violently. HM stared blankly at the wall, breathing deeply to calm himself down. The room was in the grip of silence for a few moments until HM became aware of a strange slobbering sound. He slowly turned to see Malcolm leaning on the corner of the desk, biting the back of his hand and sobbing. HM stood for a while feeling uncomfortable and embarrassed, disdainful of this snivelling mess of a man. He addressed Malcolm with chilling calm in his voice. 'I accept your resignation. I'm going to the accounts department now, and I'm going to make you out a cheque for one month's salary, plus any expenses we legitimately owe you. I would ask you to leave your office empty by the end of the day, remove any personal belongings and return your car to this office promptly at 9.30 on Monday morning, is that understood?' Malcolm nodded, without looking up, pushing his fist hard against his mouth in an attempt to staunch an incipient flood of bottled grief. HM walked from the room and closed the door on choking howls of sorrow.

Chapter 9 — THE JINGLE THAT JANGLES

Jery Hewitt was not enjoying the best of times either, and on the heels of Malcolm's, demise came into conflict with Angela Bottomly over her ideas for the Pearson's project. Angela was determined to get her own way, despite the strong support Jery had, from the media and marketing departments, over doubts about recommending television to Pearson's.

'But nationwide television advertising, apart from being unsuitable, will be far too expensive given the amount of money Pearson's can afford to spend. We would be covering too wide an audience with very short exposure in order to target a niche market, so the waste would be enormous,' Eve Merrell of media calmly informed Angela. 'These products appeal to a very specific type of person, ageing alternative medicine types who we've been successfully hitting in the magazines and health journals for many years now,' she added with all the knowledge of someone who knew this market well.

'It's all royal jelly, ginseng, and stair lifts,' Jery added, in an attempt to humorously mollify Angela's naked naïvety. Angela disliked this man who was laughingly her superior, and disdained his casual cocksure confidence. She'd soon wipe the smile from his bearded face.

'This is all stale and negative thinking!' she charged. 'Why do you suppose we're being asked to rethink Pearson's advertising? Because it stinks and doesn't work!'

'Hang on a minute, Ange, that is not so!' Jery cut in. 'It's been working extremely well. That's why M&AD has successfully kept the business for so many years. All Pearson's are asking for is an update of their magazine advertising and packaging style, no more, no less.' He was flushed and indignant at this little upstart's disparagement of other people's hard won success.

'Do not call me, Ange,' Angela said with precisely enunciated irritation. 'You have such a narrow-minded viewpoint: teeny little advertisements in health magazines don't make much of an impact. We need to broaden the market. Pearson's needs greater visibility to make it a household name. I've discussed using TV with Humphrey, and he's all for it. And I've got very good vibes about it.'

'We don't produce successful advertising on good vibes, and certainly not by discussing ideas with HM!' Jery furiously rounded on Angela. I'm the creative director around here, so consult me first please!' He'd begun to tremble, which Angela noted with mischief in her heart.

'I would have consulted you yesterday, Jery, but you were off sick, with a hangover or something, remember?' Angela replied with a sweet acid smile, 'and HM considers this a matter of great urgency if we're not to lose the business through lack of initiative.'

'Well, in my opinion, we're more likely to lose it by making costly recommendations the client cannot afford,' Eve added. 'Old man Pearson is a tricky cove, and anything that sounds over-ambitious or over-expensive will turn him right off. He doesn't take to change easily. Even HM know's that!'

'I don't think we should be making assumptions on how the client might react: we should be submitting ideas, which we believe to be in his best interests,' Angela lectured with defiant arrogance.

'I absolutely agree, but to suggest television advertising is not in this particular client's best interests.' Jery vehemently replied.

'Well I beg to differ.' Angela sharply returned.

'Fair enough then. Let's see your ideas,' Jery said, in a more conciliatory tone.

'Certainly, when they're in a presentable form,' Angela responded. 'I'm starting with a jingle first, a specially composed song for Pearson's. This will be the core on which all TV and radio commercials will be based.'

'Radio as well?' Jery spluttered.

'Yes radio!' Angela continued, 'and I've already spoken to a musician friend of mine who is the lead singer of a new band called "Eclectic Fart!"' The others looked at one another and began to laugh but Angela continued unperturbed. 'The leader of the group, as I say, is a friend of mine, Clancy Colville. He is prepared to write an original jingle for us and get the band to do a demo. If it goes well, then there'll be a fee plus the repeats. In the unlikely event that it doesn't go anywhere, then he'll just charge us a nominal demo cost.'

'And what will the nominal demo cost be?' Jery asked patiently.

'Oh, around five thousand.'

Chapter 10   CALAMITY & CALUMNY

'Five thousand pounds?'

'Humphrey, five thousand pounds is very reasonable, especially for a composer of Clancy Colville's standing,' Angela confidently replied the following morning over coffee with HM.

'But I've never heard of him!' HM said, stunned by this bombshell from his trusted protégé.

Angela smiled and attempted to reassure him with a warm huskiness in her patronising voice. 'Well that's perfectly understandable, Humphrey, but you soon will. Eclectic Fart are tipped by the music press to be big news, which can only be good for Pearson's. Think of the priceless publicity they'll get, and for free!'

HM screwed up his face as he stroked the back of his neck. It was all too much for him: he really didn't know what to think. He smoothed back his shiny Vaselined hair. 'But, Angela,' he almost begged, 'this band with this name, Electric Fart or whatever.'

'Eclectic,' she calmly corrected.

'Eclectic. One of Pearson's product lines is a laxative for pity's sake. We can't use that name!'

'I really do not see that that's relevant,' Angela said, her voice rising and her face reddening. 'It's the opportunity of a lifetime, and I've personally put a lot of time into convincing Clancy to do this for us. He's in great demand and won't work with just anyone if he feels it will compromise his art. Not using the group's proper name defeats the object of piggy-backing on Eclectic Fart's fame.' Angela stood up, ignored HM's presence, and stared towards the window with a look of saintly wonderment, as she embarked upon an evangelical soliloquy.

'A musical soundtrack written by Clancy Colville, will implant the name of Pearson's firmly in the minds of a much wider audience than the company presently enjoys. It will bring Pearson's into the twenty-first century, imbuing it with an image of modernity as opposed to the rather folksy eccentricity people tend to associate with herbal remedies. It will establish for them a platform from which to launch new lines, if they so wish, in the future. Eclectic Fart will give added value to the name of Pearson's!'

HM was fascinated by the way Angela so unabashedly quoted the name Eclectic Fart as if it were in everyday use and began to wonder, with nagging anxiety, if he might be out of step with current thinking, and if he might not be exposing to ridicule his own stale and outmoded brand of conservatism. After all, he was running a business, which is supposed to keep itself at the leading edge of market trends - according to his dictum.

'But surely any good composer can write us a successful jingle?' he suggested, in an attempt to sound reasonable. The question was certainly reasonable enough, as Angela knew, except that her 20% cash kick back from Clancy, was at stake.

'Yes, but not with the sound this band has got. It's a unique style, which people will quickly recognise and associate with Pearson's,' Angela promised, with a desperate, almost manic enthusiasm, which filled HM with unease.

'Well then, couldn't we just use this Convict chappie's name only?'

'Colville!' Angela frostily snapped.

'Er, sorry, Colville. And not use the band's name!' HM beamed at his excellent alternative. He was unwilling to upset Angela as there was something about this clever young lady, a little shorter in height than he, which fascinated and aroused him.

Angela bit her lip with a look of uncertainty, mentally weighing up the possibility of making such a concession without jeopardising her financial interest. 'Well I suppose I could ask,' she said, and HM smiled, believing he'd won the first round in a move towards a more personally acceptable compromise.

'Y' know, if this goes ahead *you* will have to be the person who presents the idea to Pearson's. You'll be better and more convincing than Jery.'

Angela relaxed back into her chair and crossed her legs slowly in front of him, smiling wickedly. 'Oh absolutely, and I'd want Clancy to be there: clients love meeting famous people.'

HM grimaced and tugged at his chin, as he stared at the floor in deep concentration. He suddenly snapped out of his reverie. 'Right then, let's do it. You'd better get things moving now, as we have to see the client very soon!'

Angela glowed, and her wide-eyed pleasure caused something to stir within HM's loins, and she knew it only too well. She stood up slowly, and as she brushed past him to leave the office he extended an arm, to gently touch her elbow.

The Besting of Humphrey Mercer

'Would you care to have dinner with me this evening, and maybe a little bubbly?' HM pulled a strange thin-lipped smile and arched an eyebrow in the most odd way. 'I've got an early meeting at Piggleford's factory tomorrow, so I'll be staying in town tonight.'

Angela's voluptuous face effused a high degree of pleasure. 'I'd love to,' she whispered, and left the room to telephone Clancy Colville with the good news.

Clancy Colville's expectation of impending fame did not exactly concur with the eulogising Angela had indulged in. He saw the Pearson's jingle project as a means of furthering his own personal financial needs, rather than funding some altruistic artistic ideal. He, like Angela, fancied some easy money, preferably at some rich old buffer's expense. But Clancy and his group's immediate requirements were more centred on the means by which to burn out more brain cells, rather than contributing to the advancement of musical excellence.

'Hi, Clancy, it's Angela. We're on. HM says we can go for it!' Angela gripped the telephone with both hands lest it should slip away.

A nasal voice at the other end of the line responded. 'Ange, wha hey you done it, thass really great doll, juss great, wait 'til I tell the boys, yeh hey cool!' Angela winced.

'Clancy dear, don't call me Ange. You know how it pisses me off!'

'Oh yeah, sorry, doll, I forgot again didn't I, iss juss I'm really chuffed. I really am, doll. You're a bleedin' genius!'

Angela laughed and brought the conversation to a conclusion. 'Alright then, let's meet up tomorrow lunchtime in the wine cellar. I've got some thoughts on a lyric we could go over.' She looked up at her closed door and continued with a whisper, 'And don't forget, I'm getting 20% out of all this, you Irish junkie.'

'Absolutely, doll, you don't wanna meet this evenin' then?'

'No, I can't,' she continued to whisper, 'that randy old roué Mercer is buying me champagne and supper tonight.'

'Ere watch it, ees after your body,' Clancy laughed, with a gravelly croak.

'Huh! I'd need a lot more than champagne before I'd let that old tosser shag me!' she replied testily.

'Better have a quick snort first then. See ya. Have a good time.'

'Bye, sweetie, see you tomorrow,' Angela mouthed kissing sounds into the telephone handset, before replacing it.

Most people found conversation with HM, on a one-to-one basis, very stilted and one sided, but Angela managed extremely well. The atmosphere in the expensive restaurant helped enormously, coupled with the fact that there was good champagne in the bucket, good food on the plate and HM was paying. He was also being uncommonly attentive to Angela's needs, and any onlooker could be forgiven for thinking that he might be in love. It was near the end of Angela's pike quenelles and HM's plump asparagus with hot butter, that "the Bollinger incident" occurred.

Amid the clatter and general hubbub of this busy venue, HM detected a distant, familiar voice calling his name. He looked up, holding the last drooping asparagus tip he was about to push into his well-buttered mouth. His face paled.

'Oh, my God,' he whispered, 'it can't be.'

'What's the matter,' Angela asked.

'Malcolm Campbell Patterson is here, and I think he's coming our way.' A very drunk Malcolm *was* coming their way, steering himself between crowded tables, lurching and bumping into waiters, until he stood at their table swaying like a tree in a gentle breeze. HM looked up, still holding his asparagus, as Malcolm addressed him rather boisterously.

'Humphrey! how the devil are you, ol' bean.'

'Hello, Malcolm, what brings you here?' HM forced an unconvincing smile from his sickly face.

'Bushiniss, ol' bean.' Malcolm was holding a fat smouldering cigar. 'I'm doing big bushiness now, brought my team here to shelebrate our fusha' shuccess.' HM thought how typical it was for this man to be celebrating today, what might not happen tomorrow. Malcolm rocked forward squinting at HM's dinner guest. 'Sh'prise sh'prise!' he shouted, 'ish our little Angie!' Angela shuddered as she looked up at this vile sweating man, wearing a maroon dinner jacket over a pale green ruffle-fronted shirt. He resembled an old hack comedian, and she suddenly visualised him in a smoke-filled club, telling gruesomely embarrassing feminist jokes to thick-legged, peroxided ladies more resembling female impersonators than housewives, as they blubbered and shook with uncontrolled mirth.

'Hello, Malcolm, how are you?' Angela returned with cool politeness. Her frozen face hardly hid her displeasure at this intrusion, and his wilfully narking misuse of her name - a sin for which she had often previously admonished him.

'Fackin' brilliant! Couldn' be better,' Malcolm dribbled, red-faced, breathing heavily as he sucked on his cigar. 'Got my own bushiness now,

The Besting of Humphrey Mercer

gonna make a fackin' forshune,' he slurred. His bright pink bowtie of the clip-on variety had turned itself sideways. 'Have my firsh million by next ether,' he croaked with laughter. 'I mean Easter.' He let forth a loud belch.

'What sort of business are you in?' HM enquired.

'Sell-synergy, of course! I'm the shole southern region agent for Beaulah Enterprises, distributors of Pershonal Attack Products.' He fumbled into his pocket and produced a crumpled business card. HM took it and read:

Malcolm Campbell Patterson (Team Leader)
Beaulah Enterprises (UK) Ltd. Under licence to
Beaulah Promotions Inc., Phoenix, Arizona, USA.

HM nodded as he returned the card.

'No, you keep it as a reminder,' said Malcolm pressing back the business card. 'You really blew out there, ol' son. Allen J never forgot me after you'd shit on me. He offered me the deal of a lifetime.' HM sensed that Allen J was probably the author of that extravagant claim. 'So you did me a big favour really.' Malcolm's attention was suddenly attracted by the drooping asparagus tip HM was still gripping in chrome asparagus tongs. 'Hey, that looks just like my dick after a night on the piss.' He shuddered with laughter. 'Don't you get any saucy ideas, Ange. Humphrey's little todger is permanently drooping. He likes a good caning though, ha, ha, ha!' Malcolm uncontrollably chortled. 'He won't be mush use to you tonight. But then little whores like you don't care as long as you get your money, eh?' Malcolm's closed eyes squeezed out fat tears as he shook with high-pitched horse laughter.

'Now you look here!' HM rounded, flushed and furious with rage. He dropped the asparagus and slid back his chair, an unfortunate manoeuvre, the floor being uncarpeted and highly polished. The chair moved back more easily than he'd expected, and his feet shot under the table, uncomfortably arching him backwards. Desperately gripping the arms of the chair in order not to slide to the floor, HM tried to heave himself up. Malcolm suddenly had one of those clear moments of inspiration which occasionally visits the alcoholic mind. With the dexterity and speed of a conjurer, he took up the Bollinger from its bucket, pulled out HM's trousers waistband and plunged the bottle upside down, deep into his 'Y' fronts.

The ululation that erupted from HM's throat would have awoken the dead in Highgate Cemetery. He had no choice but to allow himself to crash to the floor. People at surrounding tables looked on in horror as Malcolm walked away chuckling to himself. Angela jumped up to pull the gurgling bottle from HM's soaking crutch, while an anxious waiter helped him to his feet. Once upright, HM flew in pursuit. Malcolm was standing nonchalantly beside his table, boasting to his seated guests, as HM approached him at express speed. With the heroic power that only a massive shot of adrenaline can confer, HM slammed his boot into Malcolm's backside. Malcolm sprung away from the impact and fell with his full weight across the nearby dessert trolley, burgeoning with a selection of highly calorific and creamy dishes. The trolley was fitted with very large and well-oiled wheels - the merest sneeze would have moved it. With no resistance, it shot down the aisle between tables of gawping onlookers, bearing the terrified Malcolm, and crashed through the double doors which led into the kitchen. HM last saw Malcolm writhing on the kitchen floor with the overturned trolley on top of him, wallowing in profiteroles, chocolate sauce, crème brulée, gateau, cheesecake and fruit salad.

Chapter 11 — DESTINATION INFINITY

'So what did he do about his wet strides then? 'ee must 'ave looked like he'd pissed 'isself.' Clancy said, laughing helplessly at Angela's account of the previous evening.

'Well, we had to take a cab to his hotel, so that he could change while I waited in the cocktail bar. We'd only had the starter and were asked to leave - it was pathetic!' Angela said. Clancy continued crying uncontrollably with laughter. 'Oh stop it,' she snapped, with some amusement at Clancy's mirth. 'Did you snort some stuff before coming here?' Clancy tried to becalm himself, occasionally sniffing and pinching his nose between laughs. Angela poured them both another glass of house red. 'You've had a snort haven't you, you wretched junkie? What about me, when are you going to get me some more stuff?' she sharply whispered across the tannin-ringed wine bar table. Clancy ceased giggling.

'You want some more gear, doll? No probs. I'll sort some out for you, but not until you've told me what happened next.'

'Well, it was so late by the time he'd cleaned up, we finished the evening in a poxy cabaret joint, watching some third rate crooner with an orange syrup and tight trousers pulled in under his gut, singing "Delilah", surrounded by leggy bimbos. And all we could get to eat were bleeding club sandwiches.'

'Did he get 'is leg over?'

'No, he did not, you uncouth juvenile! I'm not that desperate, thank you. Besides, he was far too pissed, he could hardly stand.'

Of Irish parentage, Clancy Colville was tall, with a thick shower of mousey dreadlocks around his stubble face. His bright hazel eyes were framed with long black lashes, and he readily displayed a disarmingly pretty smile with his good white teeth, except for one missing small tooth on the right side. This, he claimed, had been knocked out by his "ol' man" during his late teens causing him to leave home vowing never to return.

He sought a career in the music business, gigged in pubs with his guitar, and worked as a dogsbody at Rivet sound studio, eventually becoming an engineer. Now at 26, he was "sort of" trying to make a name for himself with Eclectic Fart. His grubby dress style gave him the appearance of a young dosser. He had, in fact, recently moved from a squat in Hackney - where the rest of the band still resided - to a small flat, which he shared with Lily, a working girl. They did not sleep together. Lily worked nights, but liked the idea of a man being around, especially when she was working. Clancy kept the flat vaguely tidy and cooked, while Lily provided enough cash to keep them both in food. She was a pretty young girl, generous, and liked Clancy a lot; they had a sort of brother and sister arrangement which well suited both their emotional needs and lifestyles.

'We're going to have to get you something decent to wear if you're going to meet my client,' Angela said with maternal consideration.

'No thas' awlright, doll, my flatmate Lily's juss bought me some new togs for me gigs an' that, iss no problem,'

'Lily, that's a name I haven't heard for years, it's lovely, sort of old fashioned but nice'.

'Yeah, she's half Chinese or something. A real doll'.

'She must be to look after you, you little pimp!' Angela said in mock disapproval. 'Does she charge you?' Clancy shook his head with laughter, slipped Angela one of his very special spliffs and called for another bottle of red wine.

Angela arrived back at M&AD's offices rather late, and Ruth Vanderstein, the plain, but neat and tidy, receptionist called to her.

'Mr Mercer's looking for you,' she whispered.

'Oh really? I thought he was out at Piggleford's today,' Angela said, with mild concern, in her relaxed voice. 'What time is it?'

'Three-thirty. He's just this minute got back and seems to be a bit agitated. I didn't say you were out. I just said I'd page you.'

'Thanks, Ruth, give me a minute to get to my office and then go ahead and page me.'

Angela never wore a wristwatch, believing that time was an irrelevancy which could inhibit the creative flow. HM found her timekeeping very creative to say the least - especially in the morning.

HM was pacing his dark blue carpet when Angela entered his office. He spun around to face her, looking remarkably well groomed. He had that pink, sanitised look of someone who might have just come from a barbers, having had a shave, shampoo, haircut and manicure. A frown rippled his forehead. Angela, finding his scrubbed boar face highly amusing, started to giggle.

'And what's so funny?' he barked. Angela pulled her drug-relaxed mind together and offered a cheerfully obsequious explanation.

The Besting of Humphrey Mercer

'Ooh, it's just that you look so smart, not that you don't always, but you look like you've just had a haircut, shampoo and manicure.'

'I have,' he abruptly returned. 'Sit down, please.' As they faced one another, he rested his chin on folded hands and fidgeted with his feet. 'Look,' he said, quickly looking over his shoulder, in expectation of seeing the ghost of Solomon pointing in scorn. 'Look, have you said anything to anyone about Malcolm last night in the restaurant?' His bulging hard-boiled-egg eyes stared at Angela.

'No, of course not!' she boldly lied, feigning hurt and indignation that he should distrust her so. He sat back and exhaled a sigh of relief.

'I think it would be best to keep this to ourselves, don't you?' HM said sagely. Angela nodded and pointed a finger to her lips.

'Mum's the word.' Her voice was slow and earthy, and her eyes wide, with pupils dilated. She giggled again.

'So how's the jingle coming along?' HM retuned his voice to a more harmonious pitch, amused by Angela's girlie manner.

'Oh fine, er, in fact, I've not long been back from a working lunch with Clancy Colville, and we've got a rough lyric together.' She suddenly laughed heartily. The wine and narcotics were well at work in her bloodstream.

'Ah ha. May one have a look at it then?' he asked, with humour in his voice, as he leaned back with raised eyebrows and an open-mouthed grin, assuming she was flirting with him. The tip of his tongue poked out from between two wide rows of small even ivory teeth, and slid from side to side testing the keenness of their edge.

'Not quite, it's got to be fine-tuned first, and Clancy's going to put some rough music to it, so that we can get a better idea of it.' Angela was heroically controlling her desire to laugh at everything HM said.

'But Angela, I need to see something. I must have some idea of what you are going to show Pearson. A meeting is fixed for next Wednesday, which only leaves three working days. There isn't much time left!' HM spoke with sudden fierceness as he sat up and swayed forward, like a cobra about to spit venom.

'Yes I'm aware of that,' Angela happily replied. 'That's why I've arranged for us to visit Clancy after lunch tomorrow at Rivet Sound, if you can make it, of course,' she followed, with a sweet smile.

'Of course I can make it!' HM spat. He became affable once more. 'So where is this place, and what is it may one ask?'

'Rivet Sound? It's a small sound studio a twenty-minute cab ride away. You can have a pre-hear of my jingle, and perhaps we could do a spot of lunch first. There's a rather nice little bistro nearby called Monique's Kaff.' Angela looked deeply into HM's eyes, with the smile of a voluptuous

Jezebel. It was a smile, which confused him. It aroused within him a profound sexual longing, a hopelessness which reduced his authority over her. He wanted this woman, and the resolutely detached air of superiority he normally reserved for employees loosened, little by little, each time Angela and he met.

Monique's Kaff proved to be a far more agreeable little bistro than its name had suggested. Comfortable and un-ostentatiously appointed, the food was quite out of the mainstream of French style cooking, being more country kitchen than haute cuisine. The moderately priced wines were particularly good, and the patroness' stock of special cognac - copiously and generously dispensed to first-time customers by Madame Monique herself - made a deliciously effective pain killer, as HM was soon to discover.

It was in a state of Friday afternoon abandonment and relaxed affability that Angela and HM stepped from Monique's into the bright, clamouring, diesel-fumed street. Angela slipped her arm into HM's, as they teetered along the pavement and down to Rivet Sound. The studio's accommodation was a dingy warren of rooms below street level, and HM tenderly took Angela's arm as they descended well-worn York stone steps. A traumatising wail squalled from one of the small recording rooms, and a very affable young man received them as they reached the bottom of the chipped stairway. He introduced himself as "Nick the mixer", a term which baffled HM - not that he would admit as much. Nick showed them into a clean, bright office piled high with spools of tape and file boxes. A beautiful young woman with a bird tattooed on her shoulder settled them into chairs, provided coffee and explained, in an exquisitely enunciated accent, that her name was Pippa.

'Clancy will be with you shortly', she said, as the banshee torturing continued in the next room. Fortunately for HM, the full force of the volume was muffled by well-insulated walls and was doubtless reduced by the effects of too much brandy. He was enthralled by Pippa, the strange and slender young woman in whose office they were waiting. In fact, he was beginning to feel rather excited by the whole situation. The thrill of entering a subterranean temple dedicated to "musical sin" was an unprecedented experience, quite new and out of the ordinary to him, but one, which was doubtless pure routine to Angela, he thought. He savoured the illicit thrill of being in a strange place with this vibrant and talented young woman, and Monique's over-generous measures of house brandy had unhinged him a little, invoking within him a contradictory state of floating relaxation combined with highly charged excitement. The archaic expression "being with it!" entered his thoughts as he puffed one of Pippa's strange pale yellow cigarettes, while waiting for Clancy Colville to join them.

Angela, sitting opposite him, with her smooth plump legs crossed, was a vision of cherubic radiance, as she gently exhaled the thick, white smoke of a similar cigarette from her glossy full red mouth. She looked directly at HM, and he fancied that she kissed him across the foggy void between them. He sensed himself tipping backwards as a gaunt figure appeared in the smoke beside Angela. HM shook his heavy head, wondering why they were whispering. Were they whispering? Their actions seemed far too animated for quiet conversation. His eyes became heavy, as the white, strangely aromatic smoke seemed to sigh as it curled around him.

'Wait for it, wait for it, son... Now!' a bellicose commander screamed, and army cadet Humphrey Mercer was dangling over a raging torrent of reverberating foam forty metres beneath his flailing feet. His only support from a length of twisted rope was a pulley and a bar, which he gripped with the tenacity of a terrified terrier, and slid across the giddying chasm, swaying and spinning like a chrysalis hanging from a silken thread. He streaked over the deep, rocky gorge, hungry for sacrifice, and wet himself. Gasping and near sobbing he hit the far edge, welded to the bar with numb hands, and swinging dangerously, until his platoon mates hauled him to safety. The damp, dull sky was dripping chill rain, and he hoped no one would observe the steaming patch of warm urine around his fly.

'Good show, bloody good show, Humper's. You alright? The team got through with flying colours. Here, you need this.' A large glass of whisky was handed to him. The mess room was always a warm and friendly place to be in after a tough manoeuvre, but it seemed to be unfamiliarly huge and palatial. Tall and lean CO "Windy Worthington", as was printed on a label of his BD pocket, smiled in a most salacious manner. He much resembled a film actor, HM thought, the chap with the gap between his front teeth - except for the eyeliner! HM took a swig of the fiery whisky and choked on its stinging potency, as the pungent aftertaste fumed up the back of his throat and into his sinuses. He wiped his mouth with the back of his hand and Worthington laughed aloud.

'No time for cissies in our platoon,' he mocked, in a squeaky voice. His face transformed into that of a woman's. 'Come on drink it all up, Humphrey, drink it all, Humphrey, Humphrey.'

'Humphreee...,' a soft voice called at the edge of HM's consciousness, 'Humphree... Humphrey, it's Clancy!' Angela called. Clancy stood above HM wearing an ex-army battle dress jacket, which displayed a badge pinned to the pocket's flap. It bore the name Eclectic Fart. Under the jacket he wore a coarse linen collarless striped shirt with the tails hanging over the waist of his baggy brown trousers, and flower painted Doc Martin boots adorned his feet. He introduced himself to HM with his charming gap-toothed smile. HM jumped upright and sprang to attention.

He barked, as a man hypnotised. 'Present, Sah!' Pippa offered him a glass of champagne. 'No more thank you, sah!' HM mechanically responded.

Angela and Clancy ruptured themselves with laughter. HM quickly recovered from his somnolent journey and sought to rescue his dignity on the pretence of army playfulness. 'Jump to it man, come on, come on, shoulders back, chest out! And get yer 'air cut.' Blinking, bleary-eyed and satisfied that his peculiar behaviour had restored his credibility, HM slid into exaggerated bonhomie. 'Nice to meet you Clancy. I'm Humphrey Mercer. Heard so much about you, good of you to do this for us.' He hesitantly extended his hand towards this man, who probably came from another planet, as far as he was concerned. Clancy under normal circumstances would have been equally circumspect about HM, if a certain white powder, with which he was currently experimenting, had not rendered within him a universally loving frame of mind.

'Truly excellent t' see you, man Come on into the studio.' Clancy, with very dilated pupils, led Angela and HM into an empty room with black-painted brick walls, thick heavy black drapes, polished cork tile flooring and a thick Styrofoam tiled ceiling. Four padded armchairs had bunched themselves into a rough arc at one end of the room, for visitors. Microphone stands chrome-legged, clustered into a corner beside a black baby grand piano, and a hum could be heard ringing from a huge amplification system. A solitary guitar leaned against a bentwood chair, and HM took an armchair, marvelling at all of this unfamiliar paraphernalia. When all were settled, Angela presented a short rationale about the "intrinsic, motivational qualities of the jingle HM was about to experience". The ex-Rodean Pippa dispensed more chilled champagne and HM relaxed comfortably back into his deep-seated armchair, while Clancy tuned his instrument.

'Clancy's been very busy over the past few weeks but has been able to take a little time out this afternoon to play the jingle for you personally.

The Besting of Humphrey Mercer

He and the rest of the band will be laying down the final demo tracks over the weekend,' Pippa sensuously lisped to a numb, grinning and glass-eyed HM, who had not the faintest idea what she was talking about, nor did he care - he felt snug and dreamy. The huge battered Marshall 412 valve amp fizzed and cracked as jacks were unplugged and re-plugged. Clancy's fingers slid along the strings of his old Gibson "Les Paul". Bright overhead spot lamps stabbed shafts of light onto his music stand and spilled over onto a large poster on the black wall behind him. The poster's bold typesetting displayed a cryptic message in bold capitals:

ECLECTIC FART. DESTINATION INFINITY. SOLSTICE FREAKS ONLY. GLASTONBURY

Clancy pulled a microphone on its stand in front of his chair, flicked its switch with his thumb to produce a heart bursting thump, which caused a dozing HM to jerk up straight. Clancy closed his eyes, leaned back, and with a facial expression of intense grief, opened his mouth to release a nasal whining falsetto, while ripping from the Gibson's strings an overloaded backbeat.

"Kerjunga-chuck! Kerjunga-chuck! Kerjunga...

*In this world of high expectay' shun
there's a great new taste sensay' shun... you can really depen'
on this na' chrel new herb blen', cos it's the only brew,
thass pure 'an true...It must..! must must must must must must.
It must be Pearson's for yee-oo hoo hoo oo!*
(spoken) Pearson's - let's you let it all out ...yeh!"

HM was having very serious trouble focussing his tired eyes, due to the champagne, which seemed to replenish itself as fast as he could sip it, and the strange cigarettes so freely proffered by the gorgeous Pippa. The combination made him feel spongy. He at once became aware of a crackling sound and realised that he must have slipped into a few second's worth of sleep, for Angela and Pippa were clapping to a very pleased and bowing Clancy.

'Oh, sewper, well done, darling,' Angela cooed. 'We'll knock Pearson's socks off. Don't you think so, Humphrey?' she called aloud. 'I'm so pleased with the way my lyric scans so well with the music's rhythm, but then that's the skill of a good composer.' HM didn't know what to think. He smiled weakly, nodding as waves of lassitude tried hard to pull him into unconsciousness again. His age was beginning to let him down, he thought.

'Time was when this young officer could've seen off several large whiskies before lunch,' he would often boast, 'and drink several bottles of wine rounded off with a butt of crusting port, and still play a chukka of polo before the cocktail hour!' He cupped his head in his hand and massaged his forehead vigorously.

'I think I should like to hear it again, if you don't mind.'

'But you've heard it three times!' Angela said, astounded.

'No thass awlright doll,' Clancy added. 'No probs, you just relax, man, an' we'll give it another go.'

HM tried very hard to remain alert while the banal lyric was mutilated once more.

'Come on, soldjaa! lift those fuckin' feet. At the double!' HM's backpack dragged him down, and his leaden boots pulled him to his knees, as the terrifying rumble of tanks rattled across the bog ridden heath land. He was near waist deep in olive-green slime and was still sinking fast. A shrill steam train whistle pierced the smokey plain, and he was at once on the concourse of a mainline train station squinting at the destination board, which displayed characters of crisp bright capitals. He could not make any sense of them, and pondered, rubbing his chin. They did not correspond with anything familiar to him. HM couldn't even remember where he was supposed to be going, as the lady station announcer clearly enunciated the names of places he did not recognise. Between the announcements, the rumble of porter's trolleys, and the clamour of scurrying people he could just detect the strains of an old popular tune ringing from a banjo. The music was skilfully rendered by the fingers of an old soldier, propped against an iron column at the station's entrance. The soldier had various campaign medals pinned to his grubby greatcoat. His right leg was missing from the knee down, and HM stared in horror. The smiling, burning, bright eyes set in a withered white face, were those of his late grandfather.

'Now you see it, now you don't,' the old campaigner said, and was gone. HM looked above him, and his grandfather's face had transferred to a large billboard poster, advertising *Pearson's Herbal Tea!* The large grinning face held a steaming teacup to its nose and a slogan written below the face declared, 'Now *you* taste it!' A numbness pressed on HM's shoulder as he stared at the lithographed face. The faint odour of orange blossom

The Besting of Humphrey Mercer

surrounded him as the lady station announcer clearly enunciated another list of train stations he'd never heard of: Clandon, Clanky, Compo...

'Can I get you some coffee, Mr Mercer?' Pippa's radiant smile pulled into focus before HM's eyes. She was close to him and he could smell her warm lightly perfumed skin as she tapped his shoulder.

'Oh, ah yes, no thank you. I er, yes, no thank you.' Angela was looking down at him.

'You poor darling,' she tenderly whispered, 'you nodded off. You must be very tired poor love. Come on let's get you home.' HM was helped up from his chair without the slightest resistance.

'Where's Clanky compo,' he mumbled.

'Clancy? He left sometime ago, had another appointment, but he'll fix it all over the weekend,' Angela assured him.

HM, assisted by Angela and Pippa, staggered to a waiting taxi outside Rivet Sound. He was confused. Angela chattered away enthusiastically about the success of the project, and how wise HM had been in agreeing to go with Clancy, but he was still not sure what he had heard. The situation was all too new to him, even though he wouldn't admit as much, preferring to appear as knowledgeable as someone who produces advertising jingles every day.

He was not to know, however, that neither Angela nor Clancy had ever written, composed, recorded or produced a TV commercial or jingle before.

The laughter set Pearson into a fit of coughing

Chapter 12   CONFUSION WITH HERBAL INFUSION

The following Monday, HM arrived at his office looking unusually stressed and pale. His speech was at times slurred, and he'd spent a most miserable weekend feeling twitchy. His wife Elizabeth had not been happy about his unusually passive behaviour. A profound lassitude seemed to have possessed him, and he had little recollection of what had happened at Rivet Sound after lunch. He was deeply suspicious of the many strange cigarettes he'd smoked, let alone the quantity of champagne he'd quaffed. He couldn't even remember getting home, except for the cloudy memory of his chauffer finding him abandoned at some obscure country train station, sitting on a seat and crooning old Frank Sinatra songs to himself. His vascular palpitations and his ringing tinnitus increased, on discovering that Angela was not yet in her office, and he quizzed his PA.

'She's over at Rivet Sound this morning,' Stephanie Hargreave happily informed her agitated boss.

'Get her now, on my line please,' he croaked. His phone rang almost immediately and he snatched up the handset, 'Angela? What's happening, what's going on?' he questioned, with an uneasy wobble in his voice.

The Besting of Humphrey Mercer

'Morning Humphrey. Oh, you are a love. I'm so glad you called. It's all worked out beautifully. We've been here all weekend with the band, laying down the tracks, and we're now running off the final edit. Humphrey, you're brilliant. It's going to be really great!'

HM winced at her theatrical over-enthusiasm and over-familiarity. 'Er, Angela, now hold on,' HM said, as he tried hard to remain calm. 'I need to discuss this with you before we go any further. I've read the lyric again over the weekend, and I'm a little concerned. I'd like you to come back to the office right now. I want to go over a number of points with you, and perhaps get Jery's opinion. I'm just not yet fully convinced this is on the right track.'

'But you approved it on Friday! I don't believe this.' Angela's voice was shrill and on the brink of screaming. 'You told us to go ahead, and it's finished now. What are you trying to do to me?'

'Hell's teeth! What do you mean, it's finished?'

'What I've just said: we've laid down all of the tracks; we've used up all of our studio time; the studio's fully booked for the next seven days; and we're seeing the client on Wednesday. And it's fucking brilliant! Why are you doing this to me?' Angela was shrieking with tearful fury.

HM silently cursed and bit his lip. 'Yes, alright, alright, so when can we hear it?'

'I'll be bringing the finished demo in after lunch,' Angela coldly replied.

HM was still biting his lip as he replaced the phone.

For all his misjudgement, buffoonery and arrogance, HM was not one to be easily caught with his trousers down. It now seemed very sensible to have Jery Hewitt involved in creating an alternative scheme for Pearson's advertisements, based on the original request, merely as a backstop of course, he reasoned. It will enhance M&AD's standing to have a second option available at Wednesday's crucial presentation. This was essentially the line he espoused after Jery had entered his office.

'What, in case Angela's TV idea bombs out you mean,' Jery said with more than a hint of irony in his laughter.

'No, that's not it at all!' HM aggressively answered. 'Angela has produced an excellent jingle, but I would like you to demonstrate how we could update the existing advertisements for the short-term until the time is right to phase in Angela's television advertisement.' HM stared hard at Jery through bloodshot eyes. 'This will show the client that we're ahead of the game. Remember, we cannot afford to lose their business!'

'Well, would you mind telling me what Angela's TV commercial is all about, since I can't get any information from her?' Jery's attitude was turning to one of deeply vexed impatience.

'Yes, I will soon. She's bringing in a demo of her jingle after lunch,' HM said uneasily, as he pulled at an earlobe.

'Yeah, jingle, that's fine, but what's the storyline about. You can write a million jingles, but what about the visual content, what does the viewer actually see? I haven't seen a storyboard yet, have you?'

HM rolled his eyes in frustration. He was beginning to wonder if this wild idea had been thought through properly. It had not occurred to him to question the pictorial aspect of the commercial. When in doubt, when in a corner, go on the attack and change the rules immediately. This was HM's usual line of defence.

'Well, you should have! You're the creative director. I'm not in charge of the creative department, you are!' This illogical and unjust reasoning angered the usually relaxed Jery.

'But you gave the green light for this crackpot scheme! You attended the recording session, as I understand it! I wasn't consulted, and I, for one, have always been opposed to the idea. So how the fucking hell would I know what's going on!' HM variously flushed and grimaced at Jery's justifiably aggressive response, and it unnerved him a little.

'Well that may be so, Jery,' he replied, trying to calm the tension that was fast rising between them, 'but I need you to stand behind this one when we meet Pearson. I'd like you to help Angela demonstrate how versatile we can be in our approach to their advertising. I'm sure Angela's got the storyboard all worked out.'

HM needed Jery's loyalty at the moment, although he'd fall on his own sword before admitting it. Jery shrugged his shoulders and made to leave the office. He paused. 'Yeah, I get it, you're asking me to bear the responsibility for decisions that I've not been in agreement with.' With that he firmly closed the door and left HM alone and frowning, with tinnitus ringing in his ears and a flurry of confused thoughts whirling up in his fevered mind.

The Wednesday morning of the meeting with Pearson arrived so suddenly that HM awoke with a jolt. It was the sort of jolt one experiences when awakening from a deep slumber at the end of a long train journey. The light outside was brighter than usual, causing him to grab at the small alarm clock beside his bed - it fell to the floor.

'Shit!' he hoarsely whispered.

The Besting of Humphrey Mercer

'What's the trouble, Dear?' his wife murmured from the other twin bed, awoken by his commotion.

'The effing bastard alarm didn't go off! It's six thirty and I've got a presentation this morning. I'll be late!'

'Calm down, you've got plenty of time,' his long suffering wife assured him to no avail, as he went thumping and lumbering across the landing to the bathroom.

It is the opinion of many, that if your day starts off badly, it can only get worse. It would therefore be wiser to stay in bed.

Unfortunately staying in bed was not an option for HM on this occasion, if indeed any other. But it was on this day that the fates chose to give him an extra hard time: the shower ran cold; he nicked himself on the chin while shaving; his hair colorant had run out; he hadn't got time for his daily twenty minutes on the rowing machine; Eric his driver was sick today; and to put the lid on it, his soft boiled egg was hard.

'Elizabeth, four minutes, it's always four minutes for a large egg!' he whined with pained irritation on breaking open his boiled egg.

'That's right dear, four minutes for a large egg.'

'What happened?'

'What happened was that I called you three times to tell you that your egg was ready, but because you've spent so much time farting around in the bathroom your egg has got hard!' Elizabeth was unusually rattled.

HM took several long gulps from his cup and looked enquiringly at the contents. Before he could comment Elizabeth cut in.

'No, it's not tea bags, in case you're wondering.'

'No, it's coffee, is it?' he queried. 'It's rather good.'

'It's one of those Pearson's herbal tea samples you brought home and insisted on trying last night.'

'Hmm, it's jolly good.' and he drained his mug in readiness for another. He took a swig from the second cup. 'Which flavour is this one?'

'I think it was the prune 'n fig infusion, but the label was a bit damaged.'

HM choked, and sprayed hot brown liquid across the large pine breakfast table. 'Fig infusion!' he croaked.

'So?'

'Hell's teeth, woman! That's the damn laxative you've given me. Just half a cup of that's enough to blow away central London!'

'Well, how was I to know? You didn't tell me which one to make!' And don't swear just because you're angry. It won't do you any harm: these herbal things are usually quite mild.' HM left the table, wiping his mouth with a napkin, and went into the bathroom. His blood pressure was rising fast as he changed his tea-stained shirt for a clean one.

HM had to take a train to Paddington, which was running thirty minutes late, and his near apoplexy was much enhanced when the train eventually did arrive. It was packed, and the only seat available to him had been the victim of some vandals "restructuring". The seat had lost its headrest, exposing a bare metal plate, which HM's head would slap against each time the train braked. The taxi from Paddington to the office crawled through traffic jams, which seemed worse than the usually bad. 'The fates must be pissing themselves with laughter,' he hissed through gritted teeth.

'Looks like the ole' New Age travellers 'ave got 'ere before us, guv,' the taxi driver commented, when he at last drew up outside Dynamic House. The taxi stopped behind an old battered camper vehicle painted with a scattering of yellow shooting stars over a deep blue background. The legend "Eclectic Fart" was crudely hand lettered on each side of the vehicle's cabin. The exhaust pipe was hanging from strands of wire, and huge blisters of rust bubbled around the wheel arches. HM paid his fare without comment and rushed into the reception.

'What the hell is that wreck doing outside the office!' he bellowed at Ruth Vanderstein. 'I don't want that sitting there when the client arrives.'

'It's the pop group, Mr Mercer,' she replied, smiling.

'Pop group! What d'you mean pop group?'

'Morning, Mr Humphrey,' A hesitant nasal voice behind spun him around, and HM was confronted by a tall, thin, shambling and untidy figure. Clancy Colville was in his best clothes: black baggy trousers black leather waistcoat over a clean white T-shirt; and a large ex-RAF greatcoat across his shoulders, hiding a multi-coloured sequinned jacket. HM jumped back, fearing a sudden infestation of fleas from this tramp.

'Oh, huh, morning!' he answered abruptly.

'Sorry, but I 'ad t' bring the ol' van in fer the gear n' that,' Clancy explained, with his charming and familiar smile.

'Yes, well you can't leave it parked there!' HM barked, and hurriedly marched across reception and mounted the stairway to his office, where he was met by his anxious PA.

'Good morning, Stephanie. Anyone in yet?' he sharply enquired.

The Besting of Humphrey Mercer

'Good morning, Mr. Mercer. Yes, they're all the basement conference room.'

'What, my God, d'you mean the client's here already?'

'Yes, they arrived fifteen minutes ago.'

'Who, how many?'

'Two, Leslie Pearson and Mr. Pearson senior himself.'

HM shuddered at the thought of the shambling decrepit, over-opinionated Pearson senior being present with his drip of a son also. 'Have they got tea and coffee?'

'Yes,' Stephanie affirmed.

'Have you told the others, Digby, Angela Jery...?'

'Yes, they're all waiting for you!'

HM glanced at his watch. 'Oh bugger,' he cursed, 'here take my coat. I'd better go straight down. By the way, what was that damn gypsy doing in reception?'

'Well, I thought you knew.' Stephanie looked puzzled. 'He's here to demonstrate the Pearson's jingle.'

'Oh my God, yes, I'd quite forgotten.' HM clapped a hand to his forehead and closed his eyes in dismay, He turned back towards the stairs and stooped for a second. A short stab of pain pierced his abdomen. It passed quickly, and he scurried down to the basement.

HM, as always, looked exceptionally smart in his pale grey worsted wool suit, his broad blue and white striped shirt and an unusually brightly patterned tie - a birthday present from his university student daughter. It was on reaching the conference room door that he looked down at his feet for the first time that morning. He gaped with stupefaction at the ghastly blunder: he was wearing odd socks, one bright red, and the other royal blue. On such an occasion as this presentation, it was usual for HM to change his clothes several times before deciding what to wear, and he'd become confused in his panic. It was too late to do anything about it now. He'd just have to keep his feet under the table and hope no one would notice. He took a deep breath, braced himself and entered the room.

'Morning, sorry I'm late. Damn trains as usual,' HM announced to the assembled group of Angela Bottomly, Eve Merrell, Digby Hope and Jery, along with Leslie Pearson and his father. 'Mr. Pearson Sir, how nice to see you again,' HM smarmily fawned at the elderly man, who didn't visit the agency very often. When he did, he was an irritation to all with his grubby habits and embarrassingly blunt manner.

'Afternoon. Alarm didn't go off, leaves on the line, wrong kind of snow, I know, I've heard it all before,' Pearson senior responded in his usual sarcastic deadpan nasal voice. He examined the end of one of his little fingers, which he'd been gouging into his ear, and flicked something from the end of it. HM stood with a red-faced grimace of a smile, as polite hesitant laughter faintly rose from the table. Mr. Pearson senior could cause a meeting to grind on for an eternity due to his boorish and argumentative nature, but today HM believed that Angela, being a new face to Mr Pearson, would "knock his socks off" - as she would say.

Pearson senior, wearing his usual old fashioned but well tailored charcoal pinstripe suit, cut a very sober figure, with his sparse white, brushed back hair, his bulbous knobbly nose and a pair of thick-lensed glasses which magnified his small eyes to an alarming degree. A man of few excesses, Pearson senior nevertheless smoked cigarettes endlessly, making hard work for the most efficient of air conditioning systems. The fan behind the grille above him whined in protest at the rising volume of blue smoke it was barely able to cope with; thus everyone - including the majority of non-smokers - was able to share in Mr. Pearson senior's unpleasant vice.

It was also the required custom to drink Pearson's product whenever he was visiting, and he pushed a fresh pot of Pearson's dandelion coffee across to HM, who had taken a seat opposite.

'Go on; get a cup of that down yer. That'll wake you up in the morning,' Pearson senior commanded. HM could hardly refuse and managed a sickly grin, as he poured himself a cup of Dandelion 'n Chicory Breakfast Brew.

It had been one of Mr Pearson senior's many creative ideas to contract the 'and' into an apostrophe 'n' in all of his herbal tea titles, such as: Nettle 'n Borage; Fig 'n Prune; Apple 'n Mint; Rosemary 'n Buttercup etc. He felt that it gave his product a sort of modern American ring, a certain something, which would appeal to young and old alike.

'This charming young lady here tells me she's written a musical for us!' Pearson senior continued pointing to a smug Angela. 'Can't see it mesself,' he said, with a sceptical shrug.

'No, Dad, it's called a jingle,' his expensively educated son Leslie Pearson corrected.

'It's a bit early for Christmas innit!' Pearson senior shook as he cackled and croaked the familiar song "Jingle Bells". More polite laughter rippled around the table, and HM patiently waited for the performance to end, before attempting an explanation in order that this misunderstanding, as he saw it, should not drag on for too long. While a master of the obscure, humorous quip himself, HM was never sure when Pearson senior was in

The Besting of Humphrey Mercer

a joking mood, and on this occasion took the viewpoint that Pearson senior would appreciate the benefit of some further enlightenment.

'No, you see, Mr. Pearson, a jingle is an advertising expression for a musical mnemonic which is a short piece of music, with or without words, to underscore the brand...' He was interrupted.

'I know what a bloomin' jingle is, Humphrey! Don't try to explain to me something I already know,' Pearson cut in. 'But I'll tell you something you don't know: there was a van outside your office when we arrived with a couple of didicois innit. Not much old iron around here I shouldn't have thought.' He burst into quavering song again, 'Any old iron, any old iron,' and let forth another cackle, which set off a violent fit of hoarse coughing. When the fit had subsided, a liver-faced Pearson senior lit another cigarette.

'Come on then, get on with it, what've you got to show us?' He coughed smoke across the table. 'I don't want to be here all bleedin' day.'

Digby Hope, with hand over mouth, reverently whispered an "Amen" to Eve Merrell beside him.

Angela took her place at the lectern to make her case for television advertising, explaining that the fundamental basis for all future TV and Radio would be a wonderful jingle which had been especially commissioned by M&AD on behalf of Pearson's, and which had been composed by a new up-and-coming, sort of funk, rap, rock band. Mr Pearson senior sat remarkably quiet during Angela's preamble, staring at her bosom with hugely magnified eyes and a mocking grin, which she mistook for enthusiastic interest - as did HM, unfortunately. He thought that Angela had achieved the impossible, and relaxed despite the return of the stabbing pain in his abdomen.

When Angela had concluded her introduction, the lights dimmed and a coloured picture of Clancy and his motley crew of musicians appeared on the projection screen behind her. The title ECLECTIC FART was displayed above it. An expression of pained resignation spread over HM's face. She'd agreed to use Clancy's name only, he thought. Surely that was the plan. She'd clearly overlooked her agreement not to use the group's name. If only he'd fixed the deal with Clancy. He mentally admonished himself. He felt another, longer jab of pain in his stomach. Angela nodded to the small control room window at the back of the conference room, and at once a lively humming reverberated from large loudspeakers. Another button pushed by Thomas the engineer set the spools of a tape deck in motion and transmitted Clancy's nasal voice along hidden audio wires to its unerring destination. The risible lyric which had concerned HM so much burst from the loudspeakers, accompanied by the full backing of a thumping drum, growling guitars and a series of tintinnabulous electronic effects which caused Mr. Pearson senior to push his tobacco-stained forefingers into each of his ears. HM experienced another more lingering surge of pain in his abdomen; the tension was bringing on an attack of appendicitis, he concluded. Although the song lasted for about thirty seconds, it seemed like an eternity to HM, and the jingle was repeated three times with some minor instrumental change with each track. When it was over, silence ruled the room, except for the continuous sibilation from the inactive speakers. Impressive though the sound had been, nobody spoke, and concluding that all were far too impressed for words, Angela took the opportunity to introduce Clancy Colville.

'And now, Mr. Pearson, if you will allow me, I would like to introduce you to the man who made this all possible, singer, songwriter, and leader of Eclectic Fart... Clancy Colville!' Right on cue, Clancy burst through the conference room door followed by two of his grinning, unkempt musician mates carrying unplugged, electric guitars. The purging pain in HM's lower abdomen became severe as Clancy strutted to the lectern, sporting his multi-coloured sequinned jacket. Clancy turned to face the audience and took a bow. The jingle was played once more, as the grinning trio mimed and swayed to the loud, thumping rhythm. When the cacophony had ceased, Angela clapped vigorously, and someone else at the table feebly supported her applause. Mr. Pearson senior was a frozen gaping corpse. HM wriggled uncomfortably, with severely mounting abdominal pain, and as Clancy attempted to say a few words, HM involuntarily expelled a large and tuneful volume of bowel gas. A short pause gave way to uncontrollable laughter, and Clancy nervously looked in Pearson senior's direction.

'It wasn't me!' Mr. Pearson shouted, 'but whoever it was deserves a bigger round of applause. It was a damn sight more melodious than that row you lot made,' the room collapsed with laughter, and Jery Hewitt was at great pains to restrain himself from howling with mirth, 'and a sight more appropriate, if you ask me, in view of your band's name!' HM slowly moved his chair back from the table, as unobtrusively as possible, anticipating an urgent need to get to the toilet. 'Des O'Connor, that's what we need.'

'Oh, Father, really!' Leslie Pearson offered his second contribution to the meeting. 'I thought it was rather good, actually.'

The Besting of Humphrey Mercer

'Huh, you would, you bloomin' hippy.'

Smart modern-suited Leslie Pearson, who bore none of the hallmarks of his father's brain and business acumen, equally bore little resemblance to a hippy, save perhaps for his open necked, silk collarless shirt and his slightly longer than standard hair. However, to Pearson senior, whose sartorial taste would not be out of place in a firm of undertakers, such eccentric attire belonged to, as he would say, *benders and beatniks*.

HM, anticipating an argumentative dialogue between father and son, took the opportunity to disappear to the toilet. As he made for the door, his trouser legs, which had risen during sitting, did not fully drop down into place, exposing his odd socks, and Pearson senior was predictably the first to notice the error. He nudged Pearson junior with his elbow. 'Hello, look son, he's in a clown outfit also.' Pearson senior pointed to the odd red and blue socks HM was wearing and shouted, 'Are you doin' a turn next, Humphrey?'

HM felt more pressure in his gut as he reached the door. He excused himself and rapidly left the room.

'Where's the pitchers then? You can't have a TV advert without pitchers?' Pearson called after him and Angela was obliged to verbally ad-lib a visual scenario, while Pearson guffawed aloud.

When HM returned, Jery Hewitt had reached the final stages of his "second option" based on the client's original request. He had tactfully supported Angela's "interesting viewpoint", and had diplomatically got Clancy and his musicians to disappear very quickly. It was Digby Hope's skilful and timely intervention that had persuaded Mr. Pearson senior to stay for the rest of the presentation. Discussions went on into early afternoon, when Pearson senior suddenly peered at his wristwatch and abruptly announced that he must leave.

'We'll be in touch with you when we've had a chance to consider Jery's ideas,' he said, as he and his son moved from the room. HM's stomach was still in turmoil while he stood on the pavement outside M&AD seeing his clients into a taxi. On closing the car's door he dropped a fountain pen, which he'd been nervously fiddling with, and bent to retrieve it. Pearson senior thrust his head out of the cab's open window.

'D'you know, Humphrey, today is the closest I've ever come to firing your agency. I don't want to see any more electric farts.' At which, the stooping torso of HM could hardly be blamed for releasing another violent volley of wind in the direction of Pearson's face. Pearson senior was thrown hard back into his seat as the taxi sped off.

Chapter 13 — Lambs to the Slaughter

Angela Bottomly was near to tears. She bit her bottom lip and nervously jabbed a half-smoked cigarette into the ashtray on the low coffee table in HM's office. It was 6.00 p.m., HM's intestinal strife had subsided and they were taking a restorative drink together.

'I've never felt so insulted: there's no way I could work with bigots like Pearson. I didn't really want to get involved in the first place, and now you ask me to renege on our deal with Clancy. I just can't do it, and it won't do the agency's reputation a lot of good either.'

'Well, I fail to see what the agency's reputation has got to do with the fact that our client rejected Clancy's jingle,' HM replied bluntly. 'He simply preferred Jery's approach!' Being uncommonly sympathetic to Angela's humiliation, he tried to comfort her. 'But this in no way diminishes your contribution, Angela. If anything, it has elevated your standing as far as I am concerned.' Angela looked up quizzically. 'You've shown that M&AD is capable of being more versatile and creative in its approach to projects. I wouldn't mind betting that Pearson now sees us in a new light.' Angela wasn't sure of the full implication of that remark, but let it pass, assuming it to be some sort of a compliment. She then took the opportunity to trumpet her composer friend with renewed vigour.

'But Clancy's going to be big news, and an alliance with Eclectic Fart can only be good news for us. It'll be good PR for M&AD, and I care very much about our agency's reputation, Humphrey.'

HM always fell for transparent declarations of loyalty, although the reference to *our agency* disturbed him a jot. In turn, he adopted an equally transparent line in paternalism. Gingerly placing a hand on Angela's knee he leaned forward from his chair, and almost whispered, 'Absolutely right, that's why I'm simply suggesting that Clancy should waive his fee on this occasion, because there's no reason why we shouldn't use him again for a more appropriate project in the future. If it would help, I'll gladly speak to him for you.' HM spoke with barely disguised eagerness.

The Besting of Humphrey Mercer

Angela pouted at the ceiling for a moment and gently removed HM's hand from her knee. 'No, I think it better if I speak to him.' She lit another cigarette, seductively slid off her shoes and pulled her feet up into the armchair. HM watched her every move, with the look of an ageing voluptuary.

'Pour us another drink, I've got something to show you,' HM said, as he pulled himself up from his low chair and crossed the room to his desk. He opened an orange A4 folder lying on the top of some papers and removed a letter. 'Take a look at this,' he said, walking back to the occasional table, thrusting the letter before him. Angela took it from his outstretched arm and scanned the page headed:

Ayling & Slaughter International

Ayling & Slaughter was a large American owned international pharmaceutical company, which marketed many over the counter remedies: cold cures; headache pills; indigestion tablets; and various medicated ointments. They had recently acquired an old British company under the name of Dr. Byron Orgles, manufacturers of suppositories, wart remover and embarrassing-itch cream, and M&AD had previously been handling the advertising for this archaic company. The letter briefly stated that due to company restructuring, Hubert van Doren, the newly appointed European Chief Executive of Ayling & Slaughter, would be visiting M&AD to review whether or not to continue advertising, or indeed keep the Byron Orgles brands in production. He also wished to discuss whether or not Humphrey Mercer's agency would be suitable to handle any other Ayling & Slaughter business.

Angela slowly handed the letter back to HM. She'd taken little or no interest in Byron Orgles advertising to date, but now her mind became alert to new and interesting possibilities which might be open to her. She suddenly feigned disinterest and defeat.

'No, no, please not again. Jery is clearly better suited than me to work on this type of account. I couldn't face another fiasco like Pearson's. Jery will murder me if I get involved in any more of his business.'

HM was suitably moved by this "little girl frightened" sham. 'Angela, it is not Jery's business: it's the business of this agency, which *I happen to own*, and not Jery Hewitt! When a client decides to review its advertising policy, there's a good chance that the incumbent agency could lose out completely, and I cannot afford to lose out. I need you deeply involved in this review.'

'But what about Digby, Eve and the others? What are they going to think?' Angela asked, piling on the concern, clutching her gin and tonic glass with both hands and faking fear in her wide eyes.

'Neither Digby nor Eve is the creative director!'

'No, but Jery is, and I wouldn't want the client to think that I'm upstaging him,' Angela replied, maintaining her bogus distress.

'Stop worrying. None of us has met this van Doren chappie yet. He's new to us all and doesn't know Jery from Adam.' He chuckled at his pun. 'We'll bill you as a sort of creative "Agent Provocateur", who keeps us all on our toes. I'll talk to Jery, don't worry.'

Angela inwardly glowed, and a new political tactic began to shape itself deep within her sadistic and opportunist mind.

Hubert van Doren duly arrived at Dynamic House a few days later. He was a tall, continental peacock of Dutch origin, who had spent much time in the USA. As a result, he had acquired a very strange American accent, due to his high-pitched voice and distracting lisp. He wore a lilac suit over a pink shirt, finished off with a black and white polka dotted silk tie. His ash-blonde hair was immaculately coiffured - almost unreal, many thought. His thin arched eyebrows and small snub nose gave him a gnomish countenance. He smiled freely and revealed an odd habit of winking as he shook hands with the team, due to a nervous twitch. HM, acting as overall host, introduced Angela as "M&AD's new creative star". To be introduced as such pleased Angela greatly, while Jery on the other hand was quietly losing his patience. His confidence was beginning to seep away also.

Digby skilfully waffled through the routine ritual of presenting the agency's credentials - outlining the background of M&AD, the business profile and company philosophy, which was summed up with a slogan penned by HM some years earlier: *"When the chips are down M&AD spins the wheel of fortune in your favour".*

Digby always shuddered at this line, which he disliked with a loathing he found difficulty in masking, but it nevertheless educed a chuckle from Hubert. Angela beamed with approval, while the others, who shared Digby's viewpoint, inwardly cringed.

HM had zealously defended his slogan against bitter opposition, and less senior dissenters were simply threatened with termination of their employment if public lampooning or criticism of his literary skills "did not cease forthwith".

Each of the team, with the exception of Angela, made their own contribution to the meeting, which included reviewing the past advertising

The Besting of Humphrey Mercer

of Dr Byron Orgle's products and the agency's plans for the future. Jery concluded the session by delivering a short, well-reasoned piece, on the importance of re-examining Dr Byron Orgles corporate identity in the light of company changes. Jery smiled as he caught the eye of Hubert who winked at him, a sort of quiet gesture of approbation, at least, that was Jery's interpretation, so he returned the wink. He didn't know whether the man was being plain friendly or was making a pass at him; how could he tell? Hubert froze with a look of horror, mortified that anyone should so brazenly mock his unfortunate affliction. Angela, who'd remained so far silent, noted Jery's gaff with deliciously evil satisfaction.

The presentation was reaching its conclusion when, to the surprise of all, HM addressed the table with an unscheduled item. 'If I may crave your indulgence please, Mr. van Doren, I would like to call on our, er, creative trouble shooter, Angela Bottomly,' HM nervously laughed, pinching his jacket lapels between thumbs and forefingers as a proud headmaster might at a school speech day, 'er, who will relate her observations and opinions on future advertising, in order that Ayling & Slaughter is improving rather than, er, actually *ailing*.' Barely a snigger was heard, and Digby cringed at this failed attempt at humour, as HM continued with an embarrassed and reddening face. 'Angela speaks as someone new to this problem, and therefore has no preconceived notions to clutter her fertile mind.' He sat down.

Angela smiled seductively at Hubert and took her place at the lectern. The others were quietly nonplussed by this filibuster.

Jery Hewitt was inwardly fuming.

'Thank you, Humphrey,' Angela said, and paused for dramatic effect, before delivering a well-rehearsed diatribe in her shrill affected presenter's voice. There was something distinctly "Queen of England" about her intonation, which thrilled HM immeasurably. It thoroughly irritated most of the others who were obliged to listen. 'Being new to this agency, and therefore new to the Byron Orgles business, Humphrey and I thought that a viewpoint, unencumbered by past attitudes, might be of value. Having had but an hour or so to focus my thoughts, you'll forgive me, I'm sure, for any inaccuracies I may quote. What I have to say is largely "off the top of my head", so to speak.' Angela, with HM's help, had spent hours rehearsing what was to follow.

'A dramatic change is taking place in the world of Dr Byron Orgles, and if its brands are to progress into the future, all new advertising will need to be doubly effective in order to obtain a sizeable share of the market.' Digby sat staring in mute amusement at these sentiments, which seemed to be remarkably similar to those previously expressed. HM, however, hung on to every word, nodding at every sentence, as if a whole new theory on the principles of marketing was being propounded. Angela continued, 'Byron Orgles products are many and varied, and may well now be suffering from an uncoordinated advertising strategy. Even though the old-fashioned approach may have worked well in the past, it is my belief that the time is *now* for radical change before consumer interest wanes.'

Eve Merrell felt indignant at this slight on her media planning skills, and Jery felt like hitting someone or getting drunk, a pastime he was no stranger to.

'The Byron Orgle's range of products must be reviewed to see if they still meet the public's expectations, and the profitable lines should be advertised on national television and radio with a specially composed modern and memorable jingle!' Jery quietly groaned, unfortunately within earshot of HM who fixed him with a vehement narrow-eyed stare. 'The image of Dr Byron Orgles products should now conform to the Ayling & Slaughter corporate style, which means all packaging must be redesigned to this end.' Angela stood staring intently into the distance, and Jery could not help but fancy that she resembled some mythological huntress in a Ruben's allegorical study - all fleshy and milk skinned, with a head of short golden hair. Angela had stopped and the room had become as silent as a museum. Hubert van Doren suddenly stood clapping his hands.

'Thank you, Angela, thank you Humphrey,' he lisped in his peculiar American accent. 'I am particularly finding the thoughts of Angela mostly provocative. I am agreeing that the new thinking is needing, the present advertising has becoming stale, and it is my plans to instruct a change in Byron Orgle's advertising. TV is an interesting aspects of approach, and I would be happy to see what Angela can come up with before making any decisions about M&AD's future relationships, viz a viz our business.'

HM was beaming like a lighthouse as the meeting broke up for luncheon. Angela caught his eye and gave him a surreptitious wink.

'Love the company slogan,' she whispered to him, as they moved out of the conference room.

Lunch was served in the "old ballroom", as the hospitality room was referred to by the agency staff, a common quip being that a load of old balls was talked in the old ballroom. The nourishment was organised and

The Besting of Humphrey Mercer

served by Beryl Purvis, the tea trolley lady, and such an occasion as this thrilled her much, having been thwarted in her stage ambitions when a young woman. She would respond to any opportunity to "dress up" with alarming zeal, and such moments were viewed with far less enthusiasm by HM, who would shudder at the expectation of what Beryl might do to embarrass him. Uninhibited in her thespian fantasies, she would attempt to "theme" her attire to suit an important event, and this visit by the continental gentleman was an occasion which needed special consideration to Beryl's mind. Having heard that Hubert was based in France, she had thoughts of a French flavour.

The group from the morning's meeting were enjoying pre-lunch drinks in the ballroom and engaging in the usual small talk. Angela had deftly cornered Hubert and they were intently discussing TV advertising. She took every opportunity to espouse the importance of specially composed music. Jery did not stay for lunch, having an urgent problem to attend to, and profuse apologies were offered - with some discomfort on his part. HM was not the least bit concerned, and Angela was delighted. It was certain that Hubert van Doren had written him off in view of his ill-mannered impudence.

The dining table had been set with everything in place, and two flags. The French tricolour and a Union Jack crowned the table's centrepiece of red, white and blue carnations. Hubert smiled, not fully appreciating the significance of this display, when Beryl appeared carrying a long baguette. It was not so much what she was wearing that surprised everyone, but more the incongruity of such apparel on a woman of Beryl's advanced years. She was dressed in the mode of a French chambermaid.

'Bonjewer, Messewer Van Dorrin.' Beryl dropped a little curtsy, unsteady on high heels. She wore a white lace apron over a short, black skirt. She also wore a white silk blouse and a black bow was pinned to the top of her tight-permed, peroxided hair. Every mouth dropped open and HM was ramrodded with horror, looking for all the world like a corpse stiffened by rigor mortis.

'Oh, well done, Beryl, very continental indeed,' said Digby, immediately relaxing the atmosphere. He turned to Hubert. 'May I introduce Beryl, who provides our *nourriture*. Beryl is very pro-European and has clearly honoured you much by themeing your visit.' Beryl was anything but pro-European, but declined to object, as she was positively wallowing in the attention she was receiving.

'Hi, Beryl is very great honour to meet you too,' Hubert lisped in his high voice, smiling and twitching as he extended his hand. Beryl was enthralled and like Jery, mistook his nervous twitch for a flirtatious wink. HM was still in total shock.

'Charmed I'm sure,' said Beryl as she fluttered her eyelashes at Hubert. 'I hope you enjoy your lunch, Messewer. I know what you Frenchies are like when it comes to your food. I used to walk out with a young French gentlemen, you know, it was in them awful days of rationin' you know, after the second war it was and you couldn't get nylons, and…'.

'Thank you, Beryl. I think we are all ready to eat now,' HM cut in. She returned to her food preparation, while the others took their seats.

Lunch was a very pleasant: cold poached salmon; green salad; and a pureed avocado and oil dressing. Everyone took on a more relaxed mood, and the table became a buzz of chatter, accompanied by the clinking of glasses and the clack of cutlery on china. As the salad bowl was passed around, Beryl walked up behind Hubert with a silver jug containing the pureed avocado dressing. He rapidly raised his left arm to punctuate a point in his conversation, and Beryl instinctively swung the jug away from the arc of Hubert's arm, pushing its spout into the right ear of HM, sitting next to him. Cold pureed avocado flooded into HM's ear. He violently reacted by raising his elbow, whereupon a highly alarmed Beryl released the jug from her grip, allowing the entire contents to spill down the side of HM's face. The sensation of cold avocado dressing running down his ear and trickling into the collar of his shirt was an experience to be forever remembered by HM as he rapidly left the table.

Cursing, and imagining unspeakable violence against Beryl, HM stood alone in the gents' washroom, attempting to sponge green avocado stains from his collar and the shoulder of his fawn-coloured jacket. There came the sound of a toilet flushing, and from a cubicle emerged a silver-suited, blue-booted Martian. He held a full-faced, red space helmet under one arm, which bore the legend "Flash Gordon Motorcycle Couriers". The young easy-rider regarded HM's predicament for a few seconds before commenting in a sharp cockney voice.

'Bleedin' pigeons. Got no self-respect, 'ave they? They'll shit on anybody!' He left the washroom, letting forth a high stuttering laugh. His attempt at humour was not appreciated by the lone figure scrubbing at his stained Burberry jacket.

The Besting of Humphrey Mercer

Apart from the conspiracy to near ruin him, as HM viewed it, the meeting had been a great success. Hubert was impressed with Angela's attitude and requested that she "should be thinking-up" some TV jingle ideas. He also insisted that, when they were ready, Angela should bring the results to him in Paris, and all being well, he would take them to America to show his boss, Dr. Michael Vanelli, the worldwide Chief Executive of Ayling & Slaughter. HM instructed the accounts department to strike "Flash Gordon Motorcycle Couriers" off the agency's list of suppliers, but as Hubert had gallantly taken the blame for the avocado incident, an anxious and distraught Beryl was spared a grim and humiliating roasting from HM.

Angela was well pleased with the way events had turned, and Jery's absence during lunch could not have suited her ambitions better. Now, she had been given carte blanche by the client to mastermind some new ideas, and her influence over HM would be profoundly enhanced. To HM, her success with Hubert van Doren had saved the agency from losing an important client, and clearly, Jery's services were not required by Ayling & Slaughter - which made Angela a very important and valuable asset indeed. Angela needless to say, had ideas of her own. Ayling & Slaughter would serve her immediate purpose well. A large part of Angela's fury over Pearson's reaction to Clancy's jingle was due to the loss of some tax-free cash, the rest being an ego problem.

The following morning during a tête à tête with HM over coffee, Angela sought to test her power over him. She smiled as she gently sipped coffee and unravelled her new plan.

'I was just thinking,' Angela said, as she let her shoes drop from her toes and pulled her stockinged feet into the leather arm chair she occupied, 'at lunch yesterday Hubert expressed a great deal of interest in a jingle, and we've got to go to Paris soon with an idea for Byron Orgle's advertising. Now, Eclectic Fart will be finishing their first album "Destination Infinity" soon, and I know that Clancy will let me borrow an un-edited copy of it. I'll get a new jingle idea together, and we can recommend that Eclectic Fart records it for us!' Angela grinned with a look of wide-eyed innocence. HM started back from Angela, his body language showing very severe signs of a person threatened.

'Er, I'm not too sure that this would be a wise move, especially so soon after the last, er, episode.'

'No, no, we'll only pursue the idea if Hubert reacts favourably to Clancy's music. It'll be his decision entirely,' Angela eagerly assured him, 'and that way, Clancy might feel inclined to drop his fee for the Pearson music!'

HM stretched his mouth and nodded. This seemed a reasonable tactic, and although he'd personally disliked the previous music, he was prepared to accept that he might be a little out of touch with popular mass-market tastes. This was why he needed modern forward thinkers such as Angela around him, to safeguard his future interests by bringing M&AD fully into the forefront of modern advertising and marketing trends.

'Yes, well Hubert certainly was impressed with you, but we'll need to make a TV storyboard this time,' he cautioned.

'Oh absolutely,' Angela agreed, writhing with pleasure. She lit a cigarette, threw her head back and slowly expelled smoke towards the ceiling. She became thoughtful. 'Mind you, I expect if Jery had stayed for lunch, instead of rushing off, he would have got on just as well with Hubert as I did,' she said slyly, moving the conversation sideways.

'Yes, but he had an urgent personal problem,' HM mused, with little concern in his voice. 'His wife divorced him a few months ago, probably something to do with that,' HM said and took a gulp of his coffee. Angela took a long drag of her cigarette, before stubbing the rest of it in a large round white marble ashtray balanced on the wide leather arm of her chair.

'Hmm, funny that. A friend of mine saw Jery yesterday in a Mexican restaurant, La Kantina,' Angela casually murmured, while examining the long dark red nails of her left hand. 'He was apparently very drunk and was sitting and chatting with a very young man and gazing into his eyes.'

HM looked up, with an eyebrow raised in the peculiar manner he so often adopted when intrigued or aroused.

'What? Yesterday lunchtime, when van Doren was here.'

'Yes, well that's what he saw. Can't imagine what was going on, but La Kantina used to have a bit of a reputation as a hangout for rent boys you know.'

Angela and HM eventually went to France, armed with Angela's TV ideas and Clancy Colville's music for Byron Orgles new brand positioning. Hubert had previously been sent a copy of Eclectic Fart's yet unreleased first album with a signed photograph from Clancy, with which he was most delighted and had framed to display in his office. The meeting at Ayling & Slaughter's Paris office went very well for Angela. Hubert

The Besting of Humphrey Mercer

van Doren became very excited on hearing the new jingle especially composed for Byron Orgles by the talented Clancy Colville, and on viewing the trite visual ideas, neatly rendered by Reg Pewsey. All was very favourably received. HM's own opinion would have fallen far short of being flattering, but he remained politely enthusiastic. Hubert was not to know that the music specially composed for him had originally been written, albeit rejected, for Pearson's Herbal Infusions.

The afternoon meeting came to its conclusion, and Hubert hosted dinner at an excellent restaurant, along with his elegant wife - dispelling any thoughts HM had had, that Hubert might not be as other men.

It was during the toast, which Hubert proposed to Angela that he revealed his final decision. 'Well, Humphrey, this is it! To use your English vernacular, I'm thinking Angela has cracked.' Angela and HM looked alarmed. 'It's brilliant. I am personally going to take your proposals with me on my next visiting to the USA and show them to Dr. Michael Vanelli in New York. It's just polite formalities, of course. The final decisions are for me to decide. So, how you say, it's in your bag! Cheers.' Hubert raised his glass to Angela, and Angela relaxed, having now understood Hubert's amusing misquotation of 'having cracked it'.

If HM had mixed emotions over Angela's thrift in recycling the jingle, he became ecstatic over Hubert's very positive reaction and felt moved to reward Angela in some politically useful way. He proposed to honour her in such a way as to permanently secure her unswerving loyalty and eternal gratitude.

Chapter 14   Beer and Buffoonery

'Oh sewper, love it to pieces, thank you very much, Humphrey,' Angela Bottomly trilled. HM was radiating intense rapture at Angela's joy. She was quite wonderful, he thought, and her name fitted her well, being small, busty and pleasantly plumpish. The straps of her shiny red shoes criss-crossed her porcine ankles, and she emanated the promise of randy romps; that's what HM especially noticed about her - more so than observing if she actually possessed any useful talent. Angela had a coquettishness about her, which could be most charming, but her calculating intelligence endowed her with the ability to devise politically treacherous schemes on a scale which could even shame the emperor Caligula.

'And as an associate director you'll have a company car,' HM said, and his small blue eyes squinted at her ample bosom. He looked down to her ankles and up again. Angela stared into his eyes, slowly crossed her chubby legs and wriggled with satisfaction.

It had been two days since their return from the successful meeting in Paris, when HM had received a congratulatory note from Hubert van Doren, informing him that he was on his way to the USA to show Dr. Michael Vanelli the excellent TV and jingle ideas Angela had so cleverly put together. It's in the bag for sure, HM thought, as he mentally paraphrased Hubert's reference to the jingle. He had now, unwisely, rewarded Angela by elevating her status within the company, without having any idea what her new role would be.

'I think, for the time being, we'll refer to you as the creative coordinator for special projects. Yes, that's it! Creative Coordinator for special projects.' HM had struggled to think of a title for Angela which didn't sound too contrived. He did not yet wish to make her "joint creative director" as she had hinted at. It would not be wise to completely demoralise Jery. HM had justified this decision to his fellow directors by arguing that because Angela was working with Hubert van Doren at an executive level she should be made an associate director in order to give her executive status when dealing with him, or any future clients. It occurred to Digby that he'd heard that self-same justification from Angela's mouth during a previous conversation she'd had with him, when lobbying his support.

The Besting of Humphrey Mercer

Angela knew that of all the people within M&AD, HM paid more attention to Digby's opinions than anyone else. She was, therefore, at pains to gain his respect, toadying to him at every opportunity, but with less of the shameless flirting she reserved for HM.

'So, Ms Bottomly, how does this all suit you?' HM enquired, as he lecherously scanned her reclining form.

'It suits me wonderfully, thank you,' she purred. Her eyes widened, and behind the dilated jet pupils ringed with green, an infusion of treachery was gently fermenting. 'How do you think Jery will react?'

'Huh, it's of little consequence to me how he reacts!' HM barked, with a shrug of the shoulders. 'It's my decision, and that's final!' he snapped from his thin moustached mouth. He licked his dry lips and stared still and unblinking, as silent as a reptile, a stare that made Angela feel unusually uncomfortable.

It was in HM's mind that by upgrading Angela, Jery Hewitt, the official creative director of many years, might be dissuaded from seeking any increase to his salary, as well as abandoning his ambitions of joining the board of M&AD. He had never really been at ease with Jery and disliked his casual bonhomie. But Jery was very popular with everyone else. He further reasoned that Jery should remain around to fall back on, if his patronage of Angela didn't work out. Two birds in the hand are better than one in the bush, he thought.

HM frowned, as he painfully remembered quoting this ludicrous parody a year or so earlier, at the Sugden MacBrides Petfoods quarterly sales conference, when espousing the concept of putting different quantities of the same product into differently labelled and differently priced packs to increase sales. This had been the sales conference dubbed by account executive Rod Brody, as the "conference, which did *not* reach the parts other beers can".

A heat wave was on full power this July morning, and various perspiring delegates were drifting into the directors' dining room for a buffet lunch at Sugden MacBride's headquarters. A long linen covered table had been set out with an assortment of sandwiches. On a smaller table by the window, baking in the heat of the full noonday sun, were several packs of canned beer. HM sauntered into the room with Beric Reid, marketing director of Sugden's, and Beric invited a thirsty HM to help himself to a beer. HM strutted to the drinks table and, with a fawning smile, asked Beric Reid if he could get him a beer also. The marketing manager replied with his usual friendly grin that he certainly could. Whether as a result of the uncommon heat, or due to the unsettling effect of the delivery man's bone-shaking trolley, the events which followed, brought those present, close to triple hernias all round.

HM, in his bluff and pompous manner, seized a can of lager and ripped back the ring tab. The ring came away without opening the top. A gentle ripple of laughter arose from those gathering around, and HM managed a stiff smile as he shook off the ring, which had become wedged onto his forefinger. He snatched up another can. This one did open, but the pent up contents ejected before the tab was fully peeled back and, with the power of a fireman's hose, shot a cascade of froth directly between HM's eyes. Beer ran down his face and onto his military tie as he stood ramrod-backed, blinking on the foam, which dripped from his bushy eyebrows. Beric stepped forward with a napkin to sponge his face. Determined to maintain his dignity at any cost, HM violently wrenched another can from the stack while letting out a humorous mock growl. He held the can away from his face towards the window and attempted, more hesitantly this time, to open it. Perhaps over-caution was unwise. The metal ring peeled back to reveal an aperture the size of a paper punch hole before again becoming detached. The overheated pressurised contents inside spectacularly discharged through the small opening, spewing a jet of amber liquid into the louvred grille of the "Zephyr Silent Breeze Air Cooler" on the wall above.

A short high-pitched squeal from the machine gave way to a frightening BANG! and a cascade of molten metal sparks spat from the dust-laden grille, setting fire to small lumps of fluff wedged between the louvres. The machine was rendered immediately defunct as black smoke snaked from its ruined insides.

HM stood aghast and beetroot-faced.

'I thought we were going to wait 'til it got dark before the fireworks display.' Jery unwisely joked. The tension was unsprung and everyone let rip with laughter. HM's eyes narrowed at Jery, while the remaining beer, dribbling from the can, dripped down his trouser leg.

HM's eyes were still narrowed at this painful memory when Angela called him out of his reverie.

'My goodness, Humphrey, whoever it is you're thinking about, I wouldn't want to be in his or her shoes, judging from the evil look on your face.'

'Ah, sorry no, no not you,' HM lightened up, chuckled and continued, 'no , no, no, just a painful memory, but no matter. I suppose I'd better put

The Besting of Humphrey Mercer

your new position in writing now, and issue everyone in the company with a memo, eh?'

'Yes please,' Angela whispered.

Chapter 15   Queer Rumours

The memorandum from HM's office announcing Angela's new position as an associate director and creative coordinator for special projects still resides neatly folded in Digby Hope's desk diary as a memento of the events which turned M&AD's fortunes. The day the memo appeared HM had called a meeting of the board of directors in order to inform them of his intent. It was a meeting filled with bitter dissent and acrimony, as HM tried hard to assure everyone present that he was *not* encouraging Jery to leave, as Digby had suggested, but was rather "keeping him on his toes". His value was much appreciated, and he served the company well with his knowledge and ability to handle certain types of business. But M&AD needed to enhance its credibility in order to attract more "high profile clients", even at the risk of ruffling a few feathers. It seemed to Digby that he'd also heard this reasoning before and not from HM, but from Angela's mouth during another of her confidential canvassings with him. Digby also knew from experience that Angela would eventually come to grief, but at what cost to the company, he wondered. HM continued to rationalise his decision by paraphrasing Angela's well-worn sermon:

'New forward thinking is needed to advance M&AD's cause, and a specialist creative person to head up "think tank" sessions at executive level will be germane to ensuring respect from future clients. Such a move would also have the further advantage of "freeing-up" Jery, so that he can concentrate on administering the day-to-day business affairs of the creative department, without the distraction of having to attend meetings for new projects.' Digby and his fellow directors could easily guess who the original author of this plainly opportunistic and underhand rhetoric was.

M&AD's occasional chairman, the shaking Stan Molloy, contributed little in the way of opinion, save only to nod his head with a blank expression at HM's proposals - when he wasn't nodding to sleep that is. Stan Molloy's incipient senility caused him enough difficulty in remembering who Jery Hewitt was, let alone "Miss Bottom", whoever she might be, and the others knew that his opinions were about as appropriate as a sunray lamp would be, in an igloo.

The Besting of Humphrey Mercer

'But what has this woman ever done for us so far? She's got no track record apart from nearly costing us an account. She's produced nothing particularly creative except to spend five thousand pounds of company money on a risible jingle. She may be a good waffler, but she doesn't produce anything. I don't get it,' Digby said as he leaned back, staring hard at HM and pinching his left earlobe.

'Neither do I,' account executive Rod Brody added in support. 'And why should we be paying for a jingle that we can't use anyway?'

'Ah, no,' HM quietly responded, lest anyone outside the room should hear, 'we haven't paid for the jingle yet, and failed it hasn't.' HM adopted a tone of cunning confidentiality. 'Hubert van Doren is at this moment in America, showing Angela's jingle and TV ideas to Dr Vanelli, and he's certain that we'll be producing a commercial very soon. This means we can recycle Clancy Colville's work and charge Ayling & Slaughter a fortune for it, at no extra cost to us!'

'Well, you never told us. You mean you're going to use that moron's jingle for the Ayling & Slaughter project? Surely not!' Digby said, as he caught sight of Stan Molloy at the corner of his eye, nodding first up and down then from side to side, synchronising his head movements to fit whichever opinion seemed to him to be the more popular.

'No, no, well, we're using it yes! But if the client doesn't go with it this time, we'll not pay a penny piece for any of it. He'll have had two chances to prove his worth!' HM declared with the finality of one who has just pulled off a very clever coup. The others, except Stan Molloy, groaned, and Digby threw his hands into the air. 'Oh come on!' HM entreated, 'we've got to have faith in ourselves.' Digby had faith in himself well enough: his problem was having faith in the person exhorting him to do so.

The meeting was over before noon, and Digby felt obliged to find Jery and take him to lunch to mollify him before he went berserk, as he soon enough would. But Jery was in no mood for reason.

'Come on, Jery, we all know that HM's infatuated with her, but Angela will soon blow out, you'll see. Bide your time. She's a nine days wonder, like Campbell Patterson was,' Digby said across the white linen-covered table he'd reserved in his favourite French restaurant. 'HM needs you. He may own the company, but most of the clients think he's a total prat. It's people like you and me who are holding the business together, and he knows it. He can't keep you off the board for much longer. Just relax,'

'I can't, Digby. The bitch Bottomly is playing games, and I don't see why I should stand for it. I'm the creative director, and unless he fires me, I'm not going to let that little perfumed pig walk all over me. I had a wife who did that. It cost me my marriage and a lot of money.' Jery took a sip of wine and dropped back into his chair. 'HM wants to get into her knickers that's obvious enough. In fact, he's probably screwed her already.'

'No, no, he's not stupid enough to fall into that trap. Whatever one says about HM, he's a shrewd bugger. He just has his moments of total madness.' Both Digby and Jery laughed at this understatement. 'Cool it for a while. He'll drop her like a hot potato if he thinks she's putting any business at risk. Which will be soon.'

'You mean the Pearson fiasco wasn't business at risk?'

'No way.' Digby assured. 'You know old man Pearson is always threatening to leave us. Fact is no one else would want his business, and Pearson knows it, and he's an old mate of Stan Molloy.'

'Yeah, that figures. Couple of walking corpses together.' Jery squinted at the menu. 'You've got more faith than I have, Digby, but I'm still going to tackle HM about it, but don't worry, I'll keep cool. What you going to eat?' A short silence occupied their table as they both perused the menu. Food was ordered and Jery became more relaxed. A couple of glasses of burgundy had calmed him, and he felt more inclined to enjoy lunch and conversation with Digby.

Digby sipped his excellent choice of wine and reflected on the perverse turns one's life could take: how it was that when all was seemingly running smoothly in one direction, a sudden sharp bend could irrevocably change the course of events, and this day was to be no exception to that rule.

He was shaken from his reverie by a familiar voice calling his name. 'Digby! I knew it, I knew it. There you are.' Perplexed and uncertain as to where the voice was coming from, Digby looked about him confused. 'Digby, it's me!' He suddenly noticed with alarm an attractive dark-haired woman near the entrance of the restaurant waving to him. He quickly recovered his composure and wiped away the look of horror which had gripped his face.

'Good heavens, Sheila. What are you doing here?' he enquired as he rose to his feet. Sheila Piggleford quickly moved to the table he and Jery were sharing, and to his shocked embarrassment grasped him around the waist and slapped a kiss onto his mouth, as old familiar friends might.

The Besting of Humphrey Mercer

Digby furtively looked around to see if either her husband Eustace, or even Suresh Pakram, was with her. He saw nobody.

'I called in to M&AD, an' the lady at reception said you was here. I'm in town for a couple of days, doin' a bit of shoppin', Liberty's, Fortnum's that sort of thing you know. So I thought I'd look you up. Hope I'm not interrupting anythink.'

'No, no, of course not, lovely to see you,' Digby lied, with a stiff smile to hide his dismay, and introduced Sheila to Jery. 'Sheila's the wife of Eustace Piggleford of Piggleford's Pies fame,' he informed Jery, 'and Jery is the creative director who's working on the new Piggleford's packaging designs.'

'Nice to meet you, Mrs Piggleford. I must say I congratulate your husband on his good taste in women.' Jery's bold toadying caused Sheila much amusement.

'Ah ha, you smoothie, flattery will get you everywhere. Your place or mine?' Sheila broke into a lusty gravel-laden laugh. 'And plee-eese call me Sheila. So am I joining you for lunch then?' Digby's heart sank; he could hardly refuse and forced an enthusiastic grin as he pulled up another chair. 'And you're the clever artist who's goin' to make our pie packitts more attractive, certainly needs it,' Sheila said to Jery.

Digby ordered more wine and the table became a minor hubbub, occasionally punctuated by Sheila's raunchy laugh. Jery was receiving messages of sexual excitement from this bosomy and brash woman as he gained more of her attention during conversation. She had a "rude look" about her, he thought, and there seemed to be a growing empathy between them, which thrilled Jery each time their eyes met. He studied her face, and it revealed a look of longing, while her black animated eyebrows seemed to speak an enticing language of their own, re-awakening desires in this man who had been bereft of close feminine contact since the break-up of his marriage. Digby was becoming a little agitated, having had previous experience of Sheila's bizarre behaviour. Now she was here, enthusiastically quaffing every glass of wine Jery offered her. Digby was terrified that she might treat the restaurant to a performance of some kind and quietly sought ways to alert Jery of this possibility. He attempted a kind of eye language warning by first glancing at the wine bottle and nodding towards Sheila whenever she raised her glass. This was a complete failure as Jery simply misconstrued his attempts and saw them as a mute hint to ply Sheila with more wine. Digby ceased his sign language in the expectation of being able to inform Jery verbally when Sheila eventually heeded the call of nature, which she much later did, but with a little less dignity than Digby would have wished for. When Sheila rose to visit the toilet she wobbled on her high heels and fell into Jery's lap. Jery aided by a nearby waiter, carefully lifted her upright while she hooted loud, raunchy laughter.

Lunch passed without any further great embarrassment, just the bold spirited innuendo between Sheila and Jery, which, while causing no great concern, left Digby with the feeling that he was in their way. They were getting along rather well. Sheila had already revealed the name of the hotel at which she was staying, and had not been shy of including her room number within the conversation several times. But Sheila was beginning to slur sentences between her rasping bouts of laughter.

Digby called for the bill, fearing a rather more physical lesson in good relations between his lunch mate and a client's wife, and announced that, while enjoying Sheila's company enormously, he and Jery should be getting back to the office. Sheila responded by burbling that she felt sick. Jery and a waiter immediately helped her to the toilet before she could empty the contents of her stomach publicly.

During the astonishingly short while it took Sheila to re-compose herself, Digby consented to Jery's offer of gallantly escorting Sheila safely to her hotel in a taxi, and returning to the office as soon as possible. To return to the office was something Digby hoped Jery would not do, in view of his advanced state of inebriation. Jery however resolved that he would so do, as he wanted to "have things out" with HM before he left for the evening.

'Oh I am sorry,' Sheila cried in mock distress as she and Jery sat back in the taxi. Jery confidently slipped his arm over her shoulder and told her that there was nothing to be sorry about. It was something that could happen to anyone at anytime. Sheila, far from registering the faintest tremor of objection to this gentle act of familiarity, leaned her head into his shoulder and closed her eyes.

Fortunately, Jery's fitness enabled him to carefully manhandle a very limp and drowsy Sheila from the comfort of the cab when it arrived at her hotel. She leaned on him very heavily as he walked her to the hotel reception, where he asked for her key. The receptionist regarded the slouched, expensively dressed woman leaning on Jery's shoulder with grave suspicion. Jery led Sheila to the lift, pressed the ascent button and prepared to take his leave, but his politeness irked Sheila, who had begun to feel considerably improved after her short nap in the taxi. She insisted that he should accompany her to her room, and as the brushed-steel doors of the lift parted, she dragged him into the empty cabin. The bemused reception staff shrugged their shoulders and went about their individual tasks. The colour returned to Sheila's cheeks as they walked towards her hotel room. Sheila grabbed Jery's arm, squeezed it and let out her raunchy laugh. Jery was beginning to feel trapped, but felt he could not suddenly leave her alone. Once inside her room Sheila closed the door and grabbed Jery. She kissed him and, as she released him, noticed the stiff look of apprehension on his face.

'What's the matter then?' she asked, slipping off her soft leather coat and letting it drop to the floor. Jery became flustered and avoided eye contact with her.

'Look, Sheila, you're a married woman, the wife of our client, and I'm late getting back to the office.'

'Wife of your client alright,' Sheila murmured and walked to her bed. She stood silently poised over it for a moment looking weary about the eyes, then slumped flat on her back onto the large wide mattress. 'My marriage isn't exactly a bed of roses, you know.' She put her arms behind her head, lifted her legs as gracefully as a ballerina and kicked off her shoes. 'Eustace is a decent enough man, but oh I don't know, he's cold and unexciting, borin,' I suppose I'd have to say if I was honest.' The two stared at one another for a moment and Jery sat on the edge of the large bed.

'Why did you marry him?'

'Oh, I dunno. I used to be a stripper, also did a bit of singin' an' dancin' in clubs. Eustace used to come an' see me. I didn't have much of a life, wasn't making the big time. He had pots of money you know, usual story.' Sheila sighed.

'Well, at least you're still together. My wife just walked out on me, no warning,' Jery said.

'And what about your wife now,' Sheila asked.

'She's gone back to Australia and taken our son with her,' he whispered. She softly squeezed Jery's hand as he got up to leave.

'Must you go?' she whispered to Jery.

He nodded. 'See you tomorrow perhaps?'

Sheila sat up. 'Yes, come over and let me buy *you* lunch, I'll have me energy back by then!' She chuckled and kissed him, before falling back onto the bed.

'Sounds good to me. I'll call you from the front desk at one o' clock then.'

Sheila smiled and mumbled what Jery took to be an affirmative answer, closed her eyes, and drifted into sleep.

Jery watched for a taxi as he thoughtfully guided his feet along the pavement. This could be dangerous, he thought to himself, while he looked up to the leaf-shaded evening sunlight. Dusty, brown sparrows ruffled their feathers in the exhaust-laden air; starlings shrieked and clicked from the branches above the tall peeling torsos of plane trees. Jery was certainly feeling very excited at having been propositioned by an attractive woman, but also suffered anxiety over the probability of becoming embroiled in a dangerous liaison. He stuffed his hands deep into his trousers pockets and half smiled at the glowing warm sky. A stripper indeed, fancy that, he thought.

Now it was time to tackle HM.

It was 6:45 p.m. when Jery looked again at his watch while climbing the stairs to HM's office. Stephanie Hargreave informed him that HM was still haranguing the accounts manager - who'd just missed his train home - over increasing levels of out-of-pocket expenses against job sheets. Jery was comfortably ensconced in one of HM's deep leather armchairs, when the cause of his return to the office burst into the room.

'Jery! er, what's the problem? I can't spare much time. I've got to be leaving for an appointment shortly,' he briskly announced, as he ruffled some papers on his desk, avoiding the eyes of Jery, who languished in his low brown leather chair. Jery was calm and assured. He had eaten well, had taken some good wine and had flirted with an attractive woman. He was now sober enough to remain lucid and in control.

'This won't take long, Humphrey.' Jery stretched out his legs on the carpet before him and, looking up to HM stone-faced, demanded some reasons for Angela's sudden elevation. 'Explain to me why you have seen fit to promote Angela Bottomly to a position of seniority without consulting me first. I'm her boss remember?' He stared unblinking, daring a less than satisfactory reply.

HM at once became uneasy; he sputtered and would not look directly at Jery. 'Ah, er, I, well, I think I made that quite clear in my memo to everyone, er, that that's Angela's new role.' HM was decidedly discomfited by Jery's perfectly justified question and began to pace the floor. 'Her new role is part of the restructuring of this agency's new image. And Jery,' he looked down at Jery with an expression of shallow concern in his lying eyes, 'I can assure you that this decision in no way reflects on the very valuable contribution you make to our day-to-day business.'

The Besting of Humphrey Mercer

Jery smiled that "you must think I was born yesterday" smile. 'Did Mrs Bottomly tell you to say that?' he asked.

'I beg your pardon. Who? I take it that you are referring to Angela.' HM was momentarily off his guard.

'Oh come off it, you know who I mean. That's what everyone calls Angela because she bosses you around.'

'She certainly does not boss me around!' HM indignantly responded, but he hadn't been aware that she was irreverently referred to as Mrs Bottomly. It amused him a little.

'Well then, as you value me so much, make me a board director at the same time.' Jery's frankness caught HM napping again. 'Everyone agrees that the agency needs creative representation at board level, just as you have for marketing, media and the account execs. I've put this to you on several occasions in the past, and all you ever say is that you'll think about it. I think now's a good time to make a decision. I can't possibly maintain my credibility or command any authority with that woman occupying a position senior to me!'

'Now wait a minute, Jery. Angela's appointment is just on a trial basis.' HM tugged at his ear lobe. 'Let's wait and see how she works out first. I haven't overlooked your promotion at all. Trust me for a while longer and let's see how she handles things,' he said in a contrived, confidential and matey sort of way. Jery would never trust HM any further than he could throw him.

'Come on, Humphrey, don't waffle to me, give me a straight answer. Angela's manipulating you. Everyone thinks you're having an affair with her, and she's not exactly going out of her way to discourage such rumours either. It's not good for your image and could end up damaging *your* credibility.'

'Oh come on, Jery, you know as well as I do that offices are riddled with silly rumours; it's the price of being a boss. I'm surprised at you for attaching any importance to such gossip,' HM said with an abandoned shrug of the shoulders. 'After all, how would you feel if I took any notice of any rumours I may have heard about you?'

Jery was now the one taken off guard. 'Oh, what rumours might you have heard about me then?' Jery was still suffering mental sensitivity over the break up of his marriage, and was very conscious of the probability that his private affairs might be the subject of office tittle-tattle.

'Look, Jery, forget it. I'm a man of the world. It's nothing to do with me what you do in your private life.' HM was becoming nervous and evasive. 'We all have a right to respect for our privacy,'

'Come on, out with it. You're fudging again. What are you talking about? I want to know!' Jery yelled, shaking as he sat upright.

'Alright then.' HM became coldly matter-of-fact. 'You were seen in a restaurant embracing a very young man, not that I care about that, but it was at a time when you should have been here with our client from Ayling & Slaughter. You said you had an urgent problem to deal with and excused yourself from a very important lunch meeting, a meeting which Angela handled very well in your absence, as it happens'.

'What? I did have a reason. Just a minute, what the hell are you on about?' Jery blanched as a connection formed in his mind.

'A friend of Angela's saw you in La Kantina with a young man on the day of the Ayling & Slaughter visit. You were all over him crying and drunk apparently,' HM said blankly. There was a moment's silence before Jery exploded.

'That was my son! You cesspit-minded bunch of perverts! He was leaving on that day to go to away with his mother; our divorce is through and she's taking him away. I was saying goodbye. It was our goodbye lunch, you fucking, disgusting bastard!'

HM looked weakly incredulous. 'Er, oh dear, I'm very sorry.' Jery suddenly stood, tears were in his eyes and he was shaking violently.

'You can fuck off, and tell that fat little whore of yours that I'm taking legal advice immediately for slander and defamation of character,' Jery shouted, jabbing a forefinger at HM's nose.

HM stepped back a pace. 'I hardly think you'd be advised to do that. After all, under the circumstances it was a perfectly understandable misunderstanding,' HM replied, with ill-advised arrogance. He saw himself as one who had a more than average understanding of law. In fact, among his many imagined attributes, he fancied himself as a "bit of a lawyer". 'You've really got no case.'

Jery howled and moved forward. 'You're protecting that scandal-mongering bitch, aren't you?' And with a speed, which took HM by surprise, Jery's heavy fist smacked into HM's nose, spraying his shirt with blood. With the power of a gorilla Jery yanked HM's office door back, pulling it near off its hinges, and left after slamming it hard back into its jamb, splitting some panelling and sending shock waves down the corridor. He went in search of Angela, but Angela was not to be found.

Cursing with eye-watering fury, HM was relieved to find that his nose wasn't broken, as he doused his face with cold running water in the

The Besting of Humphrey Mercer

washroom basin. Most of the staff had left for the day and no one had witnessed the scene, so he hoped to keep the affair quiet, assuming Jery didn't blab about it. Anyway, he thought, Jery would be in his office tomorrow grovelling and begging to keep his job. He was in breach of his contract, and he would have to accept the situation or go. He'd make him crawl; no punishment would be great enough to atone for this indignity. The punch had bruised his ego more than causing serious physical damage, and he'd enjoy having his revenge. Angela could take over Jery's role. HM changed his blood-spattered shirt for a clean spare which he kept in the office and slipped out of the building.

The next day Jery stood in the street outside Sheila Piggleford's hotel, wondering what to do. The conflict in his mind, whether he should go in to see Sheila or just go back home, made him edgy. He had not slept well that night after his altercation with HM. The prospect of returning to a quiet empty apartment shaped his decision: he would go into the hotel's bar and order a drink over which he would decide if he should call Sheila. The large curved bar was comfortable and he ordered whisky. There were very few people around, and Jery quietly sipped his scotch, staring intently at the swaying reflections gyrating in multitudinous, scintillating patterns on the cut glass and brass at the back of the bar. He slipped into a deep melancholy.

He thought about his son, what he might be doing at this moment, and if he would be missing his father as much as his father missed him now. Jery hadn't been the best of fathers, as he'd often admitted to himself. This was largely the fault of his job. He had not been at home when fathers are needed the most. It was only a matter of time before his wife met the man with whom she would share the rest of her life.

After a second whisky he became anxious. He'd been sitting at the bar for nearly half an hour and had not made a decision about seeing Sheila. One o' clock on the dot he'd promised to call. She'd be bound to spot him in the bar if she came down in search of him. Or she might be out shopping. At one thirty it entered his mind to see her again. He paid for two large whiskies and walked into reception, feeling decidedly in a mood to see Sheila. He dialled her room number from a house phone - no answer. He dialled again and again - no success. She must be out shopping or something. She'll have left me a message, he thought, and walked to the reception desk.

'Room sixty seven, let me see.' The burgundy jacketed young man riffled through a file of cards. 'Ah yes, Mrs Piggleford has already checked out, sir.' Jery was non-plussed.

'Yes, sir.' A more senior looking manager beside the young man leaned over. He was smiling with that certain look of pleasure, which indicated that he knew something Jery didn't know. Jery recognised him from the previous evening. He'd opened the hotel door for Jery as he dragged in the limp, inebriated, Sheila Piggleford. 'I was here when she left, sir. It was quite early and a very irate lady came to collect her, her sister-in-law I believe, Peggy Piggleford. Quite an argument I must say, quite a disturbance indeed. She didn't even take breakfast. Not that it's any of my business, sir, but we run a respectable establishment here.' The man treated Jery to one of those superior sour-faced smiles, a cold expression intended to convey severe disapproval more than courtesy.

Jery wandered out into the grey damp street in a mood of hurt and confusion, his bruised ego battered again. As he wandered down the road, he thought about his day ahead. He would go home and consult his solicitor. He would write a letter to HM demanding a year's salary including a bonus, in return for his resignation. He would also write to Angela, or better still get his lawyer to do so, demanding a humiliating and fulsome apology for the poisonous slander against him.

He sincerely hoped that Hubert van Doren would fail to impress anyone in the USA with Angela's TV jingle. He reluctantly, however, accepted the probability that Clancy Colville's contemptibly laughable attempt at musical composition, might succeed this time around.

Chapter 16   Dr Michael Vanelli

Dr Michael Vanelli sat granite faced and silent, flanked on either side by two equally stone-faced executive minions who could have passed for bodyguards. He listened impassively as Hubert van Doren enthusiastically recreated the Dr Byron Orgles TV presentation Angela had made back in France. Hubert could not perhaps give it the sort of panache and edge that she had, but he made a more than plausible go of it, he thought, as he confidently lisped and twitched through the script. Hubert's mummified audience expressed not a scintilla of emotion to his performance, positive or negative, and his twitching became all the more frequent with every interminable minute's stony silence.

Hubert's meeting, straight from the airport, was a morning appointment with his American boss, who had said little throughout the whole session. The apparently mute minions said nothing either, and were asked nothing by their mogul chief.

Dr Vanelli's grave face did, however, eventually display a wince of interest when Hubert enthusiastically explained "how privileged Ayling & Slaughter was, to have an original music recorded by an about-to-hit-the-headlines English band called Eclectic Fart" and "how much immeasurable the publicity value would be to them", as he played Clancy's music from his laptop.

Relief then it was, to Hubert, when the music ceased, and the worldwide chief executive of Ayling & Slaughter suddenly produced a little black notebook and asked to know the name of the advertising agency responsible for this recommendation; doubtless wishing to personally write Humphrey Mercer a congratulatory note on his agency's ingenuity, Hubert reasoned. Clearly M&AD needed no more selling from him. To his mind Dr. Vanelli's face had taken on an aura of undiluted awe and wonderment on hearing Clancy Colville's clever jingle. As he later remarked to an office colleague, 'Mike Vanelli's thoughtful silencing spoke many volumes.'

The jingle - originally intended for Pearson's - certainly did make an impression on the worldwide chief executive of Ayling & Slaughter, who entered M&AD's name and address in his black pocketbook and rose to leave the room. He coldly, but politely thanked Hubert for his time and did not see why Hubert shouldn't return to Europe right away on the next available flight, instructing one of his wooden lapdogs to make the necessary arrangements. Despite Dr. Vanelli's restrained enthusiasm, Hubert was comfortably of the opinion that "he was cracked".

Feeling relaxed and safely airborne on his homeward flight, Hubert sipped a large gin and tonic and eventually slipped into a profound slumber. His head jogged against the cabin window as the Boeing dipped and rocked in the unstable air currents on its flight path to Europe. It was during his deep sleep that the airhostess, who had been attending to his needs, startlingly discovered something which had previously been the subject of much conjecture at M&AD. She had come to place a blanket across Hubert's knees but stopped, transfixed with wonder. Hubert's immaculately coiffured bouffant was gently sliding in small juddering increments over his left ear with the vibration of the aircraft, exposing a shiny smooth pink pate. Unfazed, and with the wisdom of the decisive person she was, the air hostess tapped Hubert's shoulder and quickly disappeared in the hope that he would awaken to reposition his expensive ash-blonde syrup.

HM remained less affected by Jery Hewitt's departure than he perhaps should have been. It was no bad thing in his opinion, and despite the disquiet of his fellow directors, paying Jery off had been worth every penny. Hubert had telephoned on his return to inform HM of how successful his meeting with Michael Vanelli had been and that he would surely be considering M&AD for some extra business.

Susanne Verdier and Dean Dalton of the creative department were well underway with the Piggleford's new package designs, and Angela was handling her new position very positively as far as HM was concerned. Occasional sackings and resignations were inevitable, and the money saved from Jery's salary allowed Angela to benefit from a more than adequate increase in her remuneration. After all, the Dr Byron Orgles business was in the bag, thanks to her. Ayling & Slaughter manufactured many other more profitable products than the Dr. Byron Orgles brand, and it now looked highly likely that M&AD would be invited to undertake the advertising for some of these more high profile brands.

The gloomy whingers who daily complained about Angela's incompetence and inability to cope were simply displaying fear and jealousy

The Besting of Humphrey Mercer

as far as HM was concerned. In time these troublemakers would knuckle down or would simply have to go, he promised Angela, a prospect which suited her ambitions very well, for she could ensure that any new recruits to M&AD would be chosen on their ability to see things more in line with her way of thinking.

For most of the people at M&AD, the real problems started when Angela acquired her new large office - or more accurately Jery's old one, expensively redecorated. Casual callers such as Clancy Colville, his fellow band members, and other motley friends of Angela's, with no particular business for being in her office other than to "hang out" and indulge in a bottle of wine along with certain smoking substances, were making life intolerable for those with work to do and deadlines to meet. HM was either unaware, or preferred to remain oblivious to Angela's gross liberties. His office was on the first floor, hers on the third, and any nuisance noise didn't affect him. Those who had urgent work to progress with Angela found it difficult to arrange meetings due to "the heavy commitments in her social diary", as George Birtles of production would often remark. The main antagonist was Angela's newly hired young personal assistant, Rosey Singleton. This beautiful, mahogany, slatternly lady with green fingernails and Cleopatra eyes had a specific remit. She kept Angela's appointments diary and ensured that unnecessary meetings - unnecessary according to her judgement - were kept to a minimum. Rosey also made certain that appointments were as difficult as possible to arrange, except in HM's case of course, for whom any task was a privilege. She carried out her policing role with great zeal and imprudence, and her lewd and crude line in backchat embarrassed even George Birtles, who was no mean exponent of lavatory humour and the unseemly metaphor.

Rosey's nostrils were also well acquainted with the white powder Clancy regularly supplied, and on most mornings she could be heard laughing wildly from HM's office while taking him through the "work in progress charts" - a new scheme introduced by Angela to ensure that her intense industry did not go unnoticed. Rosey's uncontrolled cocaine laughter was alas mistakenly interpreted by HM; he imagined that his obscure wit was the agent of Rosey's helpless mirth. He would narrow his eyes and smile at her with flared nostrils and one eyebrow oddly raised, incorrectly under the impression that he was successfully flirting. Rosey's skewed vision of him filled her with an impious sense of the bizarre. She liked to imagine how amusing it might be to sit astride this prurient pedant, and thrash him with a riding crop. Rosey was quite familiar with the secret peccadillos of old military men, having oft times supplemented her income as an *actress* in the adult movie business. To her HM was a gravy train, and she followed Angela's advice that it was in her best interests to flatter and fawn over this affluent egomaniac. She had made it clear to Rosey that his considerable wealth would yet further advantage them all. In time Angela would need a better car, Rosey would need promotion and Clancy would need more money to fund his still unsuccessful career.

Angela contemplated long and hard over whether Rosey should seduce HM, or whether she herself should become his amour. Rosey had even suggested to Angela that they should set him up for a little blackmail, and Angela had admonished the wild Rosey purely on the grounds that HM was far too wily an old bird to fall for any ploy *they* might engineer, but the idea certainly did appeal to her. For the moment Angela had a more immediate task to render, a task in which Rosey would play the leading role.

The soonerthanimagined exit of Jery Hewitt had been a gift of unexpected providence to Angela, but it had brought her into closer daily contact with the people in the creative department, especially Reginald Pewsey.

Angela's past relationship with Reg soon became a memory of loathsome regret and she would shudder at the very thought of having so enthusiastically entered into acts of intimacy with this old man her mother had so tenderly trusted. Angela feared with a real dread the possibility that her unsavoury past might become public knowledge through an incautious word from Reg when drunk. Reg was now vulnerable without Jery to support him, and Angela would feel safer if he were out of the way, so she slyly set about plotting his demise. His reputation for acts of molestation when under the influence of drink would be the key to his downfall and to Angela's thinking it would be no hard task to set him up - with Rosey's help - at the next office social event.

Angela's own birthday was imminent and birthday drinks in the nearby wine bar would be expected. Rosey's ability to tempt and tease men would be guaranteed to incite a physical response from Reg, which would give HM more than adequate justification to instantly dismiss him. After all, the old tosser was only hanging in until his pension came due. His past reputation and recent warnings about his indecent behaviour when drunk would prevent him from making claims of unfair dismissal, and so Angela took much time out to brief Rosey and think her heinous plan through.

The Besting of Humphrey Mercer

Digby Hope was daily becoming more and more concerned about the way HM was running the agency. He was concerned over Angela's lack of interest in the agency's bread and butter clients and, over a quiet drink with HM, resolved to reiterate more firmly his doubts about Angela's integrity, but before he could lodge his objections HM surprised him.

'Had a call from Eustace Piggleford earlier on,' HM mumbled quietly, while staring into his glass of pale malt whisky.

'Oh, what did he have to say,' Digby asked, draping one arm languidly over the side of his chair and twiddling his fingers inches above the dark blue, well-paced broadloom.

HM looked up forlornly from his glass. 'Wants us to put the package designing project on hold for a moment.'

'Oh! What's up then?'

'Having trouble with his wife apparently. It appears he caught her with an employee, some chemist chappie; they were at it like a couple of ferrets while he was supposed to be away. He came home unexpectedly early.'

'What? Good gracious.' Digby nervously laughed; he hadn't told HM about Jery taking a rather inebriated Sheila Piggleton to her hotel. 'Imagine that. What's it got to do with us?'

'Well, it seems that during the ensuing brouhaha, we were mentioned, well, your name in particular.'

'Wha', what the hell for?' Digby was startled.

'Don't worry; it's nothing to be concerned about. He just wondered if you knew of anything going on. It seems that while berating him for being boring, Sheila Piggleford cited your visit to Piggleford's factory as being the only exciting thing that had happened to her in years, didn't mention me though. Quite flattering for you really,' HM added, with amusement.

'Flattering! For crying-out-loud, I hope he doesn't think that I've touched her!' Digby was unusually neurotic in his manner. He knew about Jery's close encounter in Sheila Piggleford's hotel room. Digby reflected on this for a moment, then, continued in a more measured manner. 'Is he implying that I might have been messing about with his wife?'

'No, no, not at all,' HM assured Digby, 'he's not implying anything. He just wondered if you might be aware of anything that he should know about. I told him that it was most unlikely, but that I'd talk to you.'

'Too bloody right! I can't imagine why he thinks I would know anything. What a mess.' Digby poured another drink.

HM jumped up from his armchair and walked over to his desk, pulled open a drawer and lifted out a letter.

'To hell with Piggleford, for the moment anyway. Look at this. We've been asked to make a presentation to Bengt Ove Beckvorrd AB, a Swedish paint manufacturer. Got a lot of money to spend, and they're looking for a new advertising agency!' HM handed the letter to Digby. Digby put his drink down and studied the letter. His mouth fell open as his eyes flickered back and forth scanning each line several times, fearing that HM may have misinterpreted its content. But it was all there sure enough. A representative from Bengt Ove Beckvorrd, better known as BOB, would be visiting M&AD's offices within a week to give a briefing about the company, its products, its advertising requirements and available budget, etc.

'That's fantastic, Humphrey.' Digby handed the letter back, a wide grin splitting his face. 'Who's coming to see us?'

'Dunno, some boring Swedish marketing manager, I expect, but this and a possible contract with Ayling & Slaughter could put our turnover on a very healthy footing.'

'Aren't they one of Campbell Patterson's original contacts? Bit ironic to say the least,' Digby said.

HM shrugged his shoulders as he replied. 'Fuck Campbell Patterson. What if it was? He cost us enough money and I'm not about to re-hire the prat.'

'I should hope not,' Digby languidly replied, 'but if he found out, he might come sniffing around after an introduction fee.'

'Let the bugger try,' HM growled.

Chapter 17   BOB's NOT SO BORING

The Friday morning Inge Bergman stepped into the reception of M&AD every jaw dropped. She was tall, blonde and Swedish. She walked towards Ruth Vanderstein at the reception desk and announced that she had a ten o'clock appointment with Mr. Humphrey Mercer. Men passing through reception stared open mouthed.

This was the day HM had been waiting for, the visit which had been requested in Bengt Ove Beckvorrd's letter. It was for once a sunny day for HM. Stephanie Hargreave observed that he smiled the smile of a nearly human person, as opposed to the stiff-faced grimace which was more his usual expression of joy.

HM had decided to personally mastermind the BOB presentation. Acting as team leader, the personnel he gathered around him to meet Inge were naturally: Angela Bottomly, Digby Hope, Eve Merrell, Rod Brody and George Birtles - who'd hurriedly donned a jacket to hide the large patches of stale perspiration decorating the underarms of his pale blue nylon shirt. They were all assembled in the ballroom, ready to meet the representative from Stockholm.

Humphrey Mercer quickly entered reception, introduced himself to Inge and escorted her to the ballroom. He was freshly hair-coloured, manicured and summer-suited, with a pink carnation in his lapel, and he beamed with wide-eyed stupefaction as Inge shook his hand. She spoke very good English, with a slight but very pleasing accent. She was confident, polite and referred to HM as Mr. Mercer. He, attempting light humour, asked the embarrassingly obvious about her name.

'No, I am not related to the famous movie star, and before you ask, nor am I related to any Swedish film director,' she firmly replied, with a pleasant smile. It was clear enough that she wished to lay those particular questions to rest immediately.

When they at last entered the ballroom, the team were lined up along one side of the table, and HM introduced them in turn, with a brief explanation of each person's particular role. Digby Hope positively gushed and held onto Inge's hand a little longer than was necessary, to her taste, as she crushed his fingers with unexpected power in order to extricate her hand. Digby was much taken aback by her strength. HM's stiff and overly bluff manner put everyone in mind of a strutting C.O. presenting his troops to a V.I.P.

'Oh dear, I'm feeling that this is like an inspection of the Queen's soldiers, isn't it?' The others laughed nervously but were relieved that Inge had broken the tension engendered by HM's humourless and stiff formality. In a more relaxed mood, they sat around the table, and Inge introduced herself as the marketing manager of BOB. She presented the company's marketing objectives and sales strategy, while all assiduously took notes.

The task facing M&AD was to recommend an advertising plan for the launch of a new one-coat paint, currently named Schlapp-Dash, for the DIY market. The product's ludicrous brand name was the brainchild of BOB's president, Olin Andersson, who zealously defended it against bitter opposition. M&AD, nevertheless, were allowed to think of a better name and produce paint tin designs and slogans for this new one-coat paint.

Finally, it was agreed that Angela, Digby and HM would visit the plant in Stockholm in order to gain a better understanding of BOB's manufacturing methods. After this excursion, the agency would be given three weeks to present their recommendations to the BOB at M&AD's offices in London. Much to HM's relief, no mention of Campbell Patterson was ever made by Inge Bergman or indeed anyone else at BOB.

'What a bleedin' terrible name!' Dean Dalton said the following day, as Rosey handed him a copy of Angela's notes on Inge Bergman's briefing. 'I can't believe that a company like them would come up with such a naff name for a paint. I mean, they've bin around for years. Really big in the paint business.'

'Well, I never 'eard of them!' said Rosey with blunt, crude honesty.

'No, well you wouldn't. Iss all industrial paint see - cars, battleships, aircraft, y'know, heavy gear, like. Heavy duty paint, but they, like, wanna get in the D.I.Y. market now.'

'Oh, ree-elly,' Rosey replied, while chewing the nail on one of her green-tipped fingers, expressing no real concern for the subject of paint, other than nail paint.

HM stood erect in his office, gasping with wild-eyed horror. He held a heart-stopping letter from Ayling & Slaughter - a cold exercise in brevity.

The Besting of Humphrey Mercer

Dear Mr. Mercer,

Having heard the TV jingle you put forward for the Dr Byron Orgles business, I inform you that we no longer require the services of M&AD. Another advertising agency with more experience in our market has been appointed. Thank you for your interest.

Dr. Michael Vanelli

HM shook violently, as he held the thin white sheet of paper, and called for Digby, who very suddenly appeared in his office.

'Yes, I know I've heard,' Digby quickly said.

HM looked very puzzled and suspicious. 'You know about this?'

'Yes, well, I guessed. Hubert van Doren has just been on the phone to me; He's been fired by Vanelli and is blaming it all on Angela.' HM was pale; he tugged at his chin deep in thought. Digby continued, 'I'm afraid she hasn't done us any favours this time.'

'Why does everybody put the blame on Angela?' HM snapped in her defence. 'We were all part of the presentation; we're all supposed to be working as a team.'

'Yes, but we were not all in agreement over this bloody Electric Fart nonsense,' Digby angrily replied.

'Come on, Digby, we don't know that that was the reason for Vanelli dropping us. Remember that Hubert van Doren was right behind Angela on this one, and he is the client, after all. It was his decision. How were we to know?'

'Was the client!' Digby corrected, 'and I've got some more news. Eve Merrell told me this morning that she'd had a telephone conversation with Leslie Pearson, complaining that we didn't appear to be taking enough interest in Pearson's business of late, and that we are missing more deadlines than ever before!'

'Shit! Why didn't she tell me?' HM shouted, his face returning to a more familiar ruby red.

'She tried to, but you were too busy in conference with Rosey Singleton.'

'That settles it!' HM stood up. 'You and I will go to Stockholm, and Angela will have to stay here to get some action from those lazy buggers in the creative department, unless we want to lose Pearson's business as well!'

'I don't think it fair to blame the people in the creative department; they're getting no direction, no support or cooperation from Angela. She's never in on time and doesn't seem capable of delegation. The work is piling up into a serious problem, on her desk!'

'Well, I don't think you'll find that is so!' HM snapped. 'I see the work-in-progress reports. Rosey brings them to me regularly, and I can tell you that Angela is under a great deal of pressure, often having to work late herself due to the others' lack of input. She very rarely leaves the office before nine-thirty at night, you know. But I'll have a word with her and see if we can't smarten things up a bit.'

'Oh come on, Humphrey, the only pressure Angela is under is how to avoid doing any work! She's never available, apparently having more important things to attend to, and I can't think of anything more important than the business we've got at this moment, quite frankly. Lazing around in her office in the evening half stoned with Rosey, or whichever lay-about happens to call in, is hardly hard work,' Digby insisted.

HM frowned uneasily. 'Give the woman a chance please. She's only just got into the job. You'll see some action once her feet are firmly under the desk. I'll make sure of it.' HM tried to convince Digby, but Digby knew that Angela was the one who needed to smarten up.

'Yeah, well maybe someone should buy her an alarm clock,' he ruefully commented as he left the room.

HM actually smiled and nodded his agreement.

Chapter 18   Stockholm Story

It was one of those hazy warm mornings, when HM and Digby flew to Stockholm. The sun was a smudge somewhere above the thin layers of white cloud, which threatened to obliterate it completely. The plane journey was as uneventful as most air journeys are, and high above the glowing nimbostratus, HM and Digby sipped coffee, each mentally praying for a successful visit to Bengt Ove Beckvorrd. The flight took less time than they had anticipated, so they were able to first check into their hotel and still be in a taxi to BOB by lunchtime. Inge found them waiting in the reception of BOB's head office, admiring the multi-coloured striped carpet in the huge pastel painted reception area. The walls had been applied with surrealistic shapes in differing colours from BOB's paint range. She took them to the equally spacious and abstractly schemed conference room to meet the imposing Olin Andersson, and a younger man, Lars Thulman, sales director.

A light snack lunch with mineral water had been set on a large elliptical beech wood conference table, and over a fairly short break they discussed the afternoon's visit to the paint plant. Jurgen Foss, the technical director, was to be their guide despite his limited command of English - a prospect which HM and Digby found most unagreeable, having assumed Inge would be their guide.

The paint factory, a Volvo limousine ride away to the edge of town, was uninteresting. Wall to wall pigment files and silent white-coated colourists sitting at spectrophotometers contrasted dramatically, in Digby's mind, to Piggleford's pie factory. He silently admitted to himself that the pie factory visit had been far less boring. Not here the well intentioned, if misguided, enthusiasm of Oswald Pike, his ribald banter and the homely parochialism of the Piggleford's cast. White overalled men stood gloomily beside blending machines, while Jurgen Foss's dreary commentary reduced HM and Digby to mind blown, unblinking incomprehension. The afternoon ground on with interminable boredom and came to a merciful conclusion when the factory closed for the day.

Exhausted but relieved, HM and Digby were taken back to head office where examples of BOB's previous forays into the publicity arena were studied over drinks. A particular item, which Olin Andersson proudly withdrew from a portfolio, commanded much more enthusiastic attention from HM and Digby than the factory tour had. It was a calendar produced for the auto paint business. Each month featured a female model in various states of undress, holding aloft a can of BOB's auto paint. Below each glossy picture ran the slogan, "beautiful bodies are made even more beautiful with BOB's auto paint".

It was the sort of tasteless and expensively produced corn that would cause any self-respecting marketing person to writhe with embarrassment. The BOB people, however, knew that it was viewed with much favour by their auto-trade customers.

'It's all a bit of harmless fun,' Lars Thulman said, and HM flat-footedly entered into the spirit of harmless fun with a clumsy and fawning attempt at flattery.

'I must say I think Inge should have modelled for one of the calendar pictures. I'm sure she could look just as sexy as any of these supermodels, without any clothes on.'

Digby looked aghast.

'But I did,' Inge answered, without the slightest concern or hesitation. 'I posed for January and June. I used to work as a model while studying for my marketing degree.'

Olin Andersson, the large President, drained his glass and pushed his chair back.

'Well, gentlemen, I think we would very much like to see a presentation from M&AD. Perhaps in a month or so? Sort out the details with Inge. Now, please excuse me, but I should be leaving now.' He slowly elevated his tank-like bulk. 'Thank you both for your time, and I look forward to meeting you again soon.'

HM positively beamed, he suddenly jumped up. 'Oh, but I wondered if we could interest you all in dinner tonight?'

'No, no thank you, it's most kind, but my wife has arranged a small party for tonight, a relative's birthday.'

'Yes, I'm sorry, but you must count me out also, we have a new baby at home, so I must get back soon,' Lars added, 'but I'm sure Inge would be pleased to dine with two charming Englishmen.'

Inge obliged by enthusiastically replying that she would.

'In that case, I think you had better choose the venue being a native,' Digby said, thrilled at the thought of dining with a beautiful woman and not having to spend the evening alone with HM.

The Besting of Humphrey Mercer

HM and Digby tripped over each other in the struggle to disembark from the taxi first in order to hold the door open for Inge. The night was warm and perfumed with that particular leafy fragrance which pervades the air after a gentle summer shower. Well mellowed by the previous drinks, the two men were under the spell of Inge who looked striking in her simple magnolia silk dress, which contrasted dramatically with her bronze complexion.

As the trio approached the entrance to "Gaston's", two hands shot forward in front of Inge to clasp the entrance door's brass, art nouveau door handle. The hand that reached it first belonged to Digby, and in a determined effort to open the door for Inge, he mistakenly tugged hard towards himself. Inside the restaurant a large burly doorman firmly pulled the handle inwards. Digby tripped forward, and in an attempt to prevent himself from falling, instinctively grabbed HM's arm, bringing the two of them to the floor at the feet of their beautiful supper guest.

'Gentlemen, please don't fight,' said Inge with a hint of irritation. The doorman helped them up, and brushed them down.

Gaston's was a large, sumptuously appointed establishment oozing atmosphere and expense, and the mellow buzz of many people conversing and enjoying themselves greeted Inge and her two ruffled companions as they entered. On arriving at the table they had been shown to, another short scuffle ensued when HM and the waiter simultaneously attempted to pull Inge's chair out for her. The result was a sickening crack of two hard skulls meeting head on with considerable impact. Inge promptly took the seat calmly drawn out by a smug-faced Digby.

'Sometimes I think a lady can have too much attention,' she commented as she sat down.

Supper was a large platter of seafood accompanied by bottles of a most excellent Puilly fumé chosen by Digby, and of an especially fine vintage since he wasn't paying. HM, craving attention from Inge who seemed to be giving Digby more than his fair share of rapt attention, attempted to impress the Nordic vision opposite him with his knowledge of Swedish art and literature. He rambled on about the merits of the great "Swedish dramatist Ibsen" and "the influence that the play *Hedda Gabbler* had had on modern woman". He eulogised on the haunting aspect of *The Scream* by "Swedish painter Edvard Munch". Inge sat patiently and politely smiling, when Digby gently interrupted HM's bewildering discourse.

'Actually, I think you'll find that Munch was Norwegian,' HM looked at Digby fierce-faced and bulge-eyed. Inge laughed and spoke up in support of Digby.

'Yes, and so was Henrik Ibsen!' she added, with a slightly wicked smile. HM flushed and writhed with acute discomfiture.

'Ah! yes, of course, how silly of me.' Puce-faced and grimacing, HM quaffed the rest of his wine and ordered another bottle. Having made one execrable blunder, HM could always be relied upon to sink himself even deeper into the slurry of his humiliation in an attempt to exonerate himself. He just couldn't let the subject of Swedish culture rest. 'Bergman!' he suddenly shouted, *'Wild Strawberries!* So what do we think of wild strawberries?'

'I can't say I've ever eaten any!' Inge answered, 'but I would not think they would be having much flavour, eh!'

Digby was now laughing heartily, and HM wisely resolved to desist from further intellectualising.

Inge, sensing his pain, stretched out her hand and gently touched his arm. 'Well, Humphrey, you got Ingmar Bergman right; he certainly was Swedish,' she consoled. HM raised his eyebrow and gazed at her with the peculiar expression of one convinced that he might be on the brink of making a conquest.

'Thank you, gentlemen. A wonderful supper in perfect company,' Inge said, and HM called for the bill. His beaming wine face with its broad grin and mellow eyes frosted over and faded from rouge to blanc, when the waiter put the bill in front of him. Any further notions of expenditure, night clubbing or otherwise, were strictly out. Inge was tired and departed with the affirmation that they would next meet again at M&AD's offices at Dynamic House in London.

Back in London, HM organised his "plan of attack" for the grand presentation to BOB. He wouldn't trust anyone other than himself to prepare it, despite the fact that his interference in past presentations had been largely the reason for their failure. He set out his strategy and circulated it to all departments. Attached to his instructions was a telephone-directory-thick manual, on "the methods and techniques of paint manufacture", a tome which he himself would never manage to digest more than the first three pages of, believing this to be the responsibility of the marketing and creative people anyway. Their ability to recall at will, any page, was one of the many requirements contained in his brief. Everyone, of course, knew that HM would not have the slightest idea what this manual actually contained and could therefore rely on Digby Hope's ability to confabulate its contents with exemplary conviction,

The Besting of Humphrey Mercer

convincing everyone that he had digested each dreary page fully, from cover-to-cover.

Rosey knew about the secret peccadillos of old military men

Chapter 19   **DAYS OF WINE AND ROSEY**

'*Schlapp-dash!* I just do not believe eet,' said Susanne Verdier, in her pretty Parisian accent. She sat facing Angela at the newly introduced "think tank session" which included everyone in the creative department except Rosey Singleton and Reginald Pewsey. 'Eet's absolutely vomit making!' There was more than a hint of the influence of red wine in her candid attitude. Susanne, and the rest of creative department, had quaffed much Beaujolais during lunch at the local wine bar, and due to a certain event, which had occurred, were all feeling less than enthusiastic about the project before them. The

The Besting of Humphrey Mercer

lunchtime imbibing was in honour of Angela's birthday: The day of Reg Pewsey's undoing.

Angela had ensured that HM would put in an appearance to partake of a glass at around the same time the provocatively coutured Rosey would begin to seduce Reg into committing acts of indecency - his predictable failing at such gatherings. Implacably aroused by large helpings of wine and even larger helpings of Rosey's enticements, Reg was right on cue, and nobly obliged Angela with more than sufficient zeal. At the moment HM entered the wine bar, Reg was already busy sliding his hands into every available gap that Rosey's scant dress offered. It couldn't have worked any better for Angela than if she'd had a remote control button with which to manipulate Reg's alcoholically charged limbs, and she recorded sufficient evidence of his groping with her expensive mobile phone camera.

Rosey made much of the indignity by upbraiding him with foul expletives, slapping his face, and screaming attempted rape. HM quietly announced to a burbling and astonished Reg that he would speak to him later, knowing better than to publicly admonish a drunk, indignant and protesting ex-paratrooper.

'That's why we've got to think up some better names!' Angela testily replied to Susanne's cavalier condemnation of a prospective client's product. Angela, alarmed over the demise of her ally Hubert van Doren and miffed at not being included in the trip to Stockholm, had resolved to "smarten up" the creative department by giving them tasks for the weekend. 'And I want you, Susanne, to think up some new paint tin designs. I feel that your illustrative style will be especially valuable in this area.' Susanne blankly nodded, displaying as much enthusiasm for the project as a person attending a funeral. 'And I've got this absolutely stunning idea for introducing our new design,' Angela continued. 'I'm going to have someone dressed up as a giant walking paint tin, and we call the paint ToppKote. And how about this? We'll feature Mr ToppKote in a TV commercial doing a little jig!' Disbelief silenced the room. 'Well don't get so bleeding over-excited!' Angela sarcastically squeaked, indignant at the lack of enthusiasm her highly clever idea had elicited, especially after having been so generous with her birthday wine - courtesy of the petty cash box.

'A bit, as you would say, corny, eesn't it?' Susanne ventured, with a look of heart-sinking disappointment. 'That's what I call really scraping the wine cask.' Angela's face would have soured even vinegar, if it were possible. She respected Susanne's clear talent as an artist, but was less than happy about being eclipsed by her dramatic beauty. Criticism was something she did not tolerate gladly, and some form of disparaging put-down was the very least this enviously beautiful young woman deserved.

'But that's the whole point, you stupid little French tart!' Angela squawked. 'People in the paint trade are corny; they adore gimmicks, and if you can think of a better name, then get off your arse and show me. We desperately need this business, and I'll do anything to make sure we get it, so absorb that into your froggy brain, you silly slut!' Susanne was stunned into gaping silence, and Andrew Taylor gallantly took her side.

'Hey, watch it, Angela. Surely you can make your point without resorting to offensive insults. I think an apology is in order, right now!' he snapped.

Angela dismissed his reprimand with an upward jab of two fingers.

'Get to work, you lot. I'm orf out dining with the boss tonight. Tat! tah!' she said, in her mocking queenish voice, and moved to open the door. Susanne was seething. Dean Dalton shouted. ''Appy birfday,' and put two fingers up behind Angela as she left.

'Little peeg, little peeg!' Susanne hissed.

'She's getting more like "His Majesty" every day,' Andrew groaned.

'Yeah! I reckon ole' murky Mercer's givin' 'er one,' suggested Dean, in his uniquely subtle manner. 'She soon got shot of poor ole' Jery, the cow,' he reflected for a moment. 'Still, it cost bleedin' murky a few notes did'n' it.'

'Serve's the bastard right! Good for Jery,' Andrew added.

'Yeah, and now she's fuckin' gone an' done it to me,' a trembling voice echoed. They all turned slowly to see a sad dejected figure standing in the open doorway. 'Fired me that cunt Mercer has,' said Reginald Pewsey, with moist eyes.

'Reg why?' asked Susanne, alarmed.

'Sexually assaulting Rosey Singleton.'

'What? Ee can't put that one on you,' Susanne replied, with a nervously shrill laugh.

'Can't? He bleedin' *has*. An' me at fifty-nine. What am I going to do now? I can't get another fuckin' job at my age. He's fired me with a month's pay. I can't survive on that!'

'He can't, Reg. He must give you redundancy or something. You've been here for years. He can't just kick you out like that,' Andrew said, earnestly concerned. 'He's got to give you a justifiable reason.'

The Besting of Humphrey Mercer

'Sexual harassment! That's his reason,' Reg answered, grim-faced and shaking a sheet of white A4 bond. 'He had this letter typed out all ready for me. He said after continued warnings I'd persisted in harassing female members of staff and he'd heard many serious complaints against me. He said I'm lucky Rosey agreed not to prefer charges, but under the circumstances I had to go, otherwise I might face court proceedings.'

'What a load of bollocks,' Andrew responded. 'Everyone knows the little bitch was leading you on; no one takes you seriously when you've had a drink or two. Rosey's no paragon of virtue, is she?'

'I think the little cow was put up to it,' Reg said. 'I reckon she led me on so that that bitch Bottomly could get rid of me. She even took pictures of me.'

'Well, she can do without me also,' Susanne dramatically announced, and rapidly rose from her chair. 'No one calls me a tart and a slut, especially that fat-arsed, coke-snorting little peeg! I'm going to write out my resignation now. I don't need this lousy job. I am sorry, Reg.' she kissed him on the cheek and hurriedly left the room in tears.

'A dancing paint tin. Now that is a clever idea I'm most impressed.' HM said to a purring Angela. 'We'll get George Birtles to dress-up as the paint tin man; he's got nothing better to do at the moment,' he sardonically enthused, remembering that the unfortunate George was owed some punishment for his untimely remarks at the Piggleford's pie tasting. He stretched his mouth into a sinister grin and sipped the cool sauvignon, which had just been poured, as Angela and he languished in the small, quiet restaurant he had chosen for its discreet seclusion. Angela wriggled with pleasure at HM's response, and her chagrin at not having been included in the Stockholm trip was now being well compensated for by this dinner to celebrate her birthday. Success with the BOB presentation would well and truly secure her a board level directorship at M&AD, she mentally assured herself.

HM handed her a sheet of paper headed "Presentation Drill". It depicted a plan view of the conference room, over which was scattered a series of computer symbols of footprints and arrows. Two rows of chairs were arranged opposite each other. The footprints resembled the diagrams a dancing school might employ to help teach the steps of a waltz or a tango, and Angela stared at the puzzling little icons with speechless amazement.

'What do you think then?' HM asked with swelling pride. 'Good show, eh!'

'Well, er, yes, but what is it? I mean, what are these footprints for?'

'Ah, now let me explain.' HM leaned closer to Angela and gingerly placed his hand on her forearm. 'I want to conduct this presentation with military precision. You'll be commanding the creative troops while I direct the main offensive. The Swedes appreciate efficiency. We'll be well rehearsed, and each person will have a set of instructions to follow.' He lifted his hand from her arm and with his forefinger pointed out features on the sheet of paper as he revealed his scheme. 'We'll set the conference table crosswise at the back of the room for the clients to sit at. This will make a performance arena in front of them, and at each side of this area we'll set two ranks of six chairs facing inwards. The agency team, being six, will commence battle seated on the right side of the arena, in their order of presenting, the first speaker occupying the first chair in the row. As the first speaker gets up and walks to the lectern, the others move along by one seat.' HM traced a blunt finger over the arrows as he spoke. 'When the first speaker has finished, he or she exits to the left and takes the last seat in the row on the opposite side of the room.' He leaned back and gripped his jacket lapels pompously, proud of this tactical farrago.

'But what if someone should be speaking more than once!' Angela enquired, confusion crumpling her cherubic face.

'Aha, thought of that!' HM puffed out his chest like a woodpigeon at mating time. 'If someone is speaking more than once, he or she will return to the right side of the room to occupy the empty space at the end of the first line of chairs, the last occupant having moved up one chair.' His hand gently grasped her naked forearm again. Angela was at pains to comprehend HM's plan, as she frowned at the jumbled array of arrows and footprints criss-crossing the floor. She slid her arm away from his clasping fingers and spoke with a tone of patronising and long suffering patience.

'I think I can see what you are trying to achieve, but wouldn't it be less complicated to simply sit everyone around the table and let people take their turn in speaking at the lectern and return to their seats as and when required?'

'No, no, the Swedes appreciate this organised type of presentation. It's the way big companies operate.' Angela wondered where HM had got such ideas from. Certainly Digby hadn't mentioned an attitude of such formality on the part of the BOB people, and indeed, Inge Bergman had seemed quite laid-back on her recent visit.

'Well, you have the advantage over me there, Humphrey. How am I expected to know what the Swedes think. You've already met them, and I

The Besting of Humphrey Mercer

wasn't allowed to go to Stockholm, or perhaps you'd forgotten?' Angela said with clearly stated irony.

'Now, now,' HM gently chided, 'you know how desperately important it was for you to remain here and keep Pearson's happy. Let's get this business on board, then you may visit Stockholm as many times as you wish.' He lowered his voice. 'I've got plans for you, young lady.' Angela smouldered; she was intoxicated by the idea that she had saved the Pearson's business. The good wine was relaxing them both, and Angela slowly and deliberately traced her tongue around the edge of her open glossy mouth staring hard at HM. And I've got plans for me also, she mentally whispered.

He became highly excited by her look, and suddenly clapped a hand to his breast with a gasp, as one experiencing a heart attack. He withdrew from his inside pocket a small gold, foil-wrapped package and handed it to her.

'Happy birthday, my Dear,' he attempted to murmur sensually. Angela's sea-green eyes widened, as she feverishly grasped the package and tore away the wrapping to expose a small, slim red leather case. She flipped the lid open to reveal an exquisite, very expensive, solid gold and platinum wristwatch with diamonds set around the bezel. Angela gasped at its beauty, its elegance, and obvious expense.

'Oh, Humphrey, it's just beautiful. How on earth did you know I needed a watch? Thank you.' Her voice lowered, 'Thank you, Darling.' HM helped her with the catch while she put it around her wrist to admire.

'Perhaps you'll be on time in the mornings now,' he suggested, with humour in his softened voice. She laughed and kissed him on the cheek. HM reeled as he inhaled her perfume and felt the sensuous pressure of her mouth. She withdrew. 'You know, I'm very fond of you, Angela,' he said, with a faltering whisper, breathing heavily as he spoke. She smiled and squeezed his hand. It was a triumphant, snake-like smile; he was now her prey, awaiting the bite that would slowly paralyse him. Angela had got this vainglorious old buffoon exactly where she wanted him.

'Why don't you come back to my place?' Angela casually chanced over coffee, 'it's not late and I've got a couple of friends coming over for a little something to celebrate my twenty something years.'

'Ah ha,' HM said stroking his chin between forefinger and thumb, and raising his left eyebrow in the peculiar way he so often did when wishing to appear worldly and inscrutable, 'and what might this little something be, eh?' he enquired. Angela peered across the table with the eyes of an asp, her glistening mouth exposing small uncommonly pointed teeth.

'Something I think you will like very much, very much indeed,' she almost hissed. HM commanded the waiter to procure a taxi *tout de suite*, and they soon emerged onto the bustling shiny, gaudy-coloured, rain-splashed street, to their waiting transport.

During the taxi ride to Islington, Angela snuggled up to HM and brazenly rubbed her leg against his whenever the car bumped or jerked. He was becoming confused and foolish, and his body ached an old man's hunger for this young woman, this woman with the strange excitingly modern sexual attitudes he imagined she possessed.

Angela's apartment was a series of large rooms either side of a long corridor, and HM found himself in a huge Victorian lounge, spacious with high corniced ceilings, and filled with voluminous soft furnishings, haphazardly shoved around the edges of a polished, bare-boarded floor. A thick yak-skin rug lay in the central area, on which stood a low white marble table. On the table, a fat stumpy aromatic candle burned atop what appeared to be a wax-dribbled skull. An open package of marijuana and several skins of Rizla paper were lying around it. The lighting was extremely dim, and various demonic figurines revealed themselves at points around the room through the pale haze of herbal smoke, lethargically floating around him like aromatic ectoplasm. Joss sticks smouldered from flower vases, while an eerie chanting music moaned from somewhere in the background. HM was both thrilled and a little frightened, standing in what seemed to be a den of decadence and profanity.

'You cheeky little tart,' Angela trilled to a deep armchair in the far corner of the room. Spirals of bluish smoke emerged from its depths. 'You've started without me.' The chair laughed a familiar husky laugh, two long black silky legs, bent at the knees, slowly straightened as a flimsily clad brown figure stood, with glass of champagne in one hand and a smouldering twist of yellowed paper in the other. HM blinked towards the mahogany ghost, his eyes becoming adjusted to the dimness. Josephine Baker, he thought.

'Hello, Humphrey,' Rosey said, with an oily sexiness which startled him, 'so you've come to join the fun and games.'

'Come along then,' commanded Angela, as she slapped Rosey's protruding posterior, 'get my guest and me a glass of champagne; it is my birthday after all.' Rosey disappeared to the kitchen and HM felt even more uncomfortable. He hadn't expected Rosey to be here and was uneasy at her frank familiarity, apart from her extremely transparent apparel. He suddenly thought about the unfortunate Reg Pewsey.

The Besting of Humphrey Mercer

'Come on, let me take your coat, make yourself comfortable and relax,' Angela cheerily said, planting a soft kiss onto HM's cheek. He caught a waft of her delicate perfume again, and his unease began to dissolve, as he recalled the kiss she'd given him earlier. He sat down into a low spongy armchair, which almost enveloped him, as Rosey reappeared, carrying a tray loaded with two large flutes and a bottle of chilled Bollinger. She knelt at his feet and adopted the passive manner of a handmaiden, as she poured champagne and presented him with a selection of small canapés. He was soon feeling less threatened and approved of Rosey's subservience. He was on his second glass when Angela drifted back into the room. His mind raced with conflicting emotions. She now wore a short white silk robe, which clearly outlined her soft, plump, naked form beneath. He caught himself staring open mouthed, and quickly took another swig of champagne, emptying his glass, which was promptly replenished by Rosey.

'Oh, my gracious, what service,' he chortled. I must say, it's very good bubbly.' HM winced just a little, as he moved to ease his well fed, corseted abdomen.

'I told you you'd like it,' Angela said standing over him. She bent down to loosen his tie. 'Come on, relax,' she said and gently massaged his neck, as he twisted his head to either side.

'Ooh, ah, that's very nice,' he grunted, and he thought he heard a distant bell tinkling as he rocked with the motion of Angela's kneading fingertips.

'Come on, slave girl,' Angela called to Rosey, 'take over. I've got guests to welcome.' HM tried to protest, but Rosey countenanced no heed to his resistance and promptly sat astride him with her chest at his face, as she continued the manipulation of his tensed neck muscles.

'Ooh, you feel really stiff,' she impudently whispered, and HM released a raucous laugh. A moment later Angela re-entered the room with a man and woman. HM regarded the white suited, crop-haired man over Rosey's shoulder. He gripped HM's hand with the familiarity of someone who knew him well. But HM could not place him. The woman looked like an oriental prostitute, as far as he could tell; he wasn't wrong for she was Lily. He didn't recognise Clancy without his locks, and never did remember who he was for the rest of that evening.

The night was filled with champagne and exotic smoke. Rosey was firmly ensconced in HM's lap, her long legs draped over one side of the chair and her arm around his shoulder, while the quiet and lingering tintinnabulation of strange music shifted around the room. Other bodies seemed to disappear and reappear from the smoke-shadowed doorway, as Rosey fed HM little puffs from her handmade cigarette. He was feeling relaxed, and again *with it,* but he mentally resolved to keep his foggy wits about him. He was enjoying the feel of Rosey wriggling on him, as she moaned to the magnetic music, and at times he fancied he heard his name whispered somewhere in the mournful shadows, but paid little heed. HM was becoming divinely unconcerned by anything occurring around him; his attention was centred on the delightful Rosey, as she blatantly flirted and caroused with her employer. He took another long drag from the cigarette Rosey was holding for him, and felt a pressing sensation on top of his head. Rosey leapt from the chair with the dexterity of an acrobat and pulled HM to his feet.

They were suddenly dancing, or at least moving in a kind of rhythm which resembled dance, as he stiffly goose-stepped around Rosey, who was swaying and flailing her arms, rooted to the floor and bending like a willow sapling in a breeze. The muffled vibration of heavy rock music pumped into his ears. Other writhing shapes filled the room. HM was overheating. He removed his jacket and flung it somewhere. Rosey slid her spider-leg fingers into his shirt, and they gyrated, clinging, to the dizzying beat. HM felt as one sleepwalking.

Angela's grinning face suddenly appeared above his head, and he wasn't sure whether he was upright, horizontal, awake or dreaming, all sense of proportion seemed to have no logic.

'Go on boy, you're next!' The command was barked at HM as he took his place under the showers, alongside a row of naked young male bodies. 'You've got two minutes, so make it snappy.' The soap shot from his hand and disappeared slithering through pairs of wet and soapy feet. He noted with alarm that some of the feet had painted toenails, and he remembered having been told never to bend over in the shower room. He let the soap go.

HM stood erect, cold and unclothed, as the steel-eyed school medical officer scrutinised him, He stared with alarm at the MO's shadowed face, whose eyes were outlined with blue mascara. Intermittent blinding flashes stabbed through high windows, a thunderstorm, he thought, as a rumbling sound settled dull and muffled onto his ears.

'Ever had the clap, boy!'

'Er, no, sir,' the young HM replied.

'Anything horrible like that?'

'No, sir.'

The Besting of Humphrey Mercer

The scarlet-mouthed MO leered and winked. HM drifted into a dormitory with piles of clothing haphazardly strewn over beds. A boisterous young man leapt onto his back, stabbed his heels into his buttocks crying, 'Gee-up, old horse.'

'It's like trying to flog a dead camel,' another young blade yelled, with a very odd high-pitched laugh, and more lightening burst through blackened windows. Humphrey tripped and fell flat onto his face, and his giggling rider tumbled on top of him; other bodies tumbled onto him and all breath was forced from his lungs.

Suddenly, silence.

HM gingerly opened an eye. He was flat on his back, in a low-lit bedroom. It was quiet and empty. Muffled chattering bubbled somewhere along the corridor outside. He became aware of Angela by the door pulling on her robe. Rosey was standing naked beside her, tapping the side of her thigh with a riding crop. Both were silhouetted by the backlight glowing from the passage.

'Had a good sleep then?' Rosey cheerfully asked, as she playfully whacked his leg with the crop. He shook his head and was astonished to find that he was also naked.

'Wha, wha what happened,' he burbled.

'You've been flat out and flaccid for the past hour,' Angela curtly replied, lighting a cigarette.

'Shit, where are my clothes?' He sat up and looked wildly about him. His trousers were roughly thrown over a chair, his shirt was on the floor and he saw, with blood-draining dismay, the girdle he wore to hold in his belly, thrown over the bedside lampshade. 'Call me a taxi quick!' he demanded.

'You're a Taxi!' Rosey screamed with laughter at her predictable quip. Angela sniggered, while HM returned panic-stricken to a fuzzy form of sobriety. He could not imagine what had happened, but his main intent was to get dressed and out of Angela's flat as fast as his jelly-like legs would allow. He attempted to stand but buckled at the knees. The two women helped him to his feet. His head thumped with the blows of several hammers and he was feeling nauseous. He called for a glass of water, which Rosey promptly delivered along with a fizzing seltzer tablet.

'I expect it was something you had for dinner,' she inappropriately remarked, giggling as he drained the foaming brew. He heaved, pushed her to one side, snatched up his trousers and headed, hopping, for the toilet. He passed a seedy looking man wielding a camera.

'Alright, mate?' the dark-glassed snapper enquired, and HM elbowed him to one side. When he later emerged, somewhat relieved but shivering, Angela presented him with the rest his clothes and helped him dress. He vehemently denied any knowledge of the corset, claiming that it must be someone else's. It certainly was not his!

Rosey called a taxi.

In the back of the warm cab, he massaged his head in an attempt to ease the sponginess and nausea, which gripped him, as he tried to remember what had happened during the evening. He wondered how he came to be in a state of undress. That cool, eerie primeval glow which precedes sunrise was seeping up into the horizon when he arrived home. The few stars still hanging above him, as he crept to his door, were fading. Being mindful not to wake Elizabeth he gently slid into his bed and passed out.

George Birtles attempted to step out the Toppkote jig

Chapter 20   Musical Chairs

'So what does Digby think about your presentation plan for Bengt Ove Beckvorrd?' Angela asked, all bright and smiling, as HM, looking very nervous and grim faced, scanned a list of new names and slogans for Schlapp-dash.

'Digby can think what he likes, as far as I'm concerned. The agency is facing a financial crisis, so be assured that what we present to BOB, and how we present it, will be *my* decision,' HM sternly replied, as he took a sip of his coffee and shuddered. He'd arrived at the office late, had felt bad over the weekend and hadn't slept at all well. He felt totally drained of all energy after the Friday night experience, of which he remembered very little. Fragments of imagery tantalisingly flitted through his brain: Angela's pink form; Rosey's mocking face; and crashes of blinding light. There were also recollections of Angela's distinctive perfume, the rise and fall of raucous laughter. Rosey's nubile, naked form. He assumed the visual images to be the result of bizarre dreaming during his fitful weekend slumbers.

He was twitchy in his movements, and fearing eavesdroppers, walked to his office door, opened it, looked down the corridor and, satisfied that nobody was around, closed it. He returned to his seat.

'Ah, listen, Angela!' he quietly said, 'er, about Friday evening.'

'Shush, don't worry,' she reassured, 'you didn't do anything.' He relaxed, relieved. 'Not for the want of trying, of course,' she pointed out. He sat up straight again with a pained and startled glare. Angela put a forefinger to her mouth, and he saw, with dismay, the expensive watch he'd bought her in a moment of ill-considered spontaneity, a moment he'd quite forgotten. 'Stay cool, nothing will pass these lips, I assure you,' she added, in a whisper. 'It's our little secret.'

'Er, that girl of yours, Rosey, she'll have to go!'

'But why?'

'Too dangerous to have around,' HM said, with a sharp whisper.

'But you told her that her services were indispensable, and that you were going to see that she got a raise in salary. You're being most unfair; she wouldn't tell a soul, believe me; she'll do whatever I tell her,' Angela forcefully pleaded. It was a series of statements, which gave him little comfort, and he rolled his eyes like a man insane on learning of his promise to Rosey, a promise he could not remember having made.

'Please, don't shout!' he spat.

'I'm not shouting,' she whispered.

'Then tell her that she should look for another job immediately. Your future depends on it, and remember,' an oily smile oozed from his pallid face, 'directors sometimes have to make unpleasant decisions.'

'I'd like to get the Swedish presentation completed first, for which I need Rosey's help. We've only a week or so to go now,' Angela said, and paused for a second or two. 'You know she might think that you're a bit of a racist if you're not careful.'

HM's eyes bulged as he hissed through clenched teeth. Fearing an embarrassing revelation concerning his unwise moments of stupidity, he reluctantly agreed that Rosey could stay until after the BOB presentation.

By now people within the agency were lampooning HM's footprint plan, referring to it as "strictly come dancing" or "musical chairs". Within

The Besting of Humphrey Mercer

days of zero hour, HM called a team meeting to discuss progress, and to make some final adjustments to the presentation. During his opinionated lecturing, much to everyone's relief, he was called away by Stephanie to take an urgent telephone call. When he had left the room, Dean and Andrew stood to perform a parody of the planned ToppKote paint tin dance, while Susanne called out directions from HM's presentation drill plan. The others were cheering loudly when the familiar sound of someone clearing their throat became audible above the jollity. The dancing couple froze in mid twirl. HM stood in the doorway with a stiff grimace freezing over his face. He slowly moved into the room.

'Well, I must say I'm glad to see that some of you have found something to laugh about,' he acidly remarked, 'but you'll all be laughing on the other side of your faces when I tell you that Pearson was on the phone. We've lost his business! So you'd all better make bloody sure we win this one!' He slammed the door on leaving.

Angela was not amused

The Friday morning of the presentation to Bengt Ove Beckvorrd arrived with alarming speed. Weeks of soul-searching, argument, writing, designing, rethinking and rehearsing, had all too rapidly passed, resulting in a presentation which everyone was highly nervous about, not because of any doubt about the effort put in, but more the result of failing faith in HM's military choreography, which had proved so chaotic at rehearsals. Furthermore, the spontaneous burst of uncontrollable laughter George's clumsy attempt at dancing aroused, while wearing the replica of a giant paint tin, had severely upset Angela. She'd been far too sensitive to appreciate any humour at this stage of the game, especially in light of Susanne's resignation, which had humbled her into a lengthy apology and an expensive lunch, intended to encourage Susanne to stay at least long enough to help her through the BOB presentation. The loss of Pearson's had reduced Angela's credibility and her influence over HM was dangerously close to being neutralised. HM's reputation for suddenly going off people in a big way made Angela uneasy. A contingency plan would need to be concocted.

The prospective clients from Stockholm were expected to arrive at 10.30 a.m. It was certain the meeting would continue through lunch, and Beryl Purvis was instructed to provide an assortment of sandwiches, fresh fruit and drinks for one-thirty precisely. She was also commanded to refrain from indulging in any further embarrassing amateur dramatics. HM's footprint floor plan continued to worry those involved in this much needed new business pitch, except HM himself.

At 10.15 a.m., HM, sporting a new pair of thick black-rimmed spectacles, descended the stairs to check the basement presentation room and see that everything was in order. George Birtles was in the kitchen with Beryl, trying on his giant cardboard paint tin, which bore the name "ToppKote". He was still not used to walking in it, even after many rehearsals. The resultant howls of laughter his jigging had caused secretly pleased HM immeasurably, his perverse satisfaction at George's humiliation spreading across his face like the grin of a medieval torturer. This, indeed, would constitute the punishment George deserved for his impudent behaviour during the Piggleford's pie tasting.

Angela was not in the least bit amused.

'Geddit then?' George said to Beryl, as he peered through the two eyeholes cunningly hidden within the lettering.

'No, I can't say I do,' said Beryl, frowning.

'Top coat, y' know, like overcoat. Top paint, one coat, protective, it's a "dooblee ontonder".' Beryl wasn't convinced that she understood what he was blathering on about, as it was especially difficult to relate to someone talking from within the muffling confines of a giant cardboard

The Besting of Humphrey Mercer

cylinder. George continued his cardboard prattle, 'And you should see the advertising slogan bleedin' Mrs. Bottomly's come up with: "*Smart guy's only do it once with ToppKote*", yuk!'

It was Angela who had dreamed up the name ToppKote and the winning slogan. She had ensured that HM chose her ideas, over far better contributions from the other creatives, by not letting him know who'd written what, and by systematically demolishing the better efforts with mystifying rhetoric masquerading as logic. HM was eventually moved to unprompted and gushing approval of the name ToppKote and its pisspoor slogan. He had suggested "perhaps GreatKote, instead of ToppKote ", a change which Angela vehemently vetoed. Only when having elicited HM's approval, did she admit to having been the author of this trite piece of advertising copy.

HM's furious bespectacled face suddenly appeared at the kitchen door. 'What the hell are you doing?' he croaked. George spun around knocking Beryl against the tea trolley, which was set out with a tray of freshly washed cups and saucers. The trolley crashed, clinking, into the wall to the detriment of its cargo. 'For chrissake, man, the clients will be down here in a moment. You'll give the whole goddamn game away!' HM squeaked, and his new spectacles slid to the end of his nose. 'Get out! For godssake, hide quickly,' he shouted to the cardboard cylinder as he pushed his glasses back up. Everyone knew that HM's new reading aids were a blatant emulation of Digby's optical apparel, but sadly they did not imbue him with quite the same intellectual charisma. Furthermore, the thickness of the lenses magnified his small pupils, causing his eyes to appear all the more bizarre when he became enraged.

Muttering incantations and shaking her head at HM's uncontrolled blasphemy, the seriously religious Beryl set about replacing the broken crockery.

Olin Andersson, Lars Thulman and Inge Bergman arrived right on cue, to find the presentation team uncomfortably seated in a row of chairs along the wall at the right side of the room. As the visitors took their seats behind the large table, a whining noise could be heard issuing from an air conditioning grille above - at HM's insistence the motor had been set to maximum to ensure the room didn't grow stuffy. HM straightened his tie, cleared his throat and took his place first at the lectern. He introduced the proceedings with a nervous, thin-voiced introductory address.

'Lady and gentlemen, ah ha, I, er won't introduce myself to you again, er, as you've doubtless seen enough of me already.' The merest snigger at this feeble witticism was heard from somewhere among the shadowed faces before him. 'Thank you for this opportunity to make our, er, representations for the Bengt Ove Beckvorrd advertising account.' He was having difficulty in seeing his notes properly and paused. 'Lights!' he surreptitiously hissed from the side of his mouth. Digby, the next in line to speak, had forgotten to depress the button on the panel behind him, which operated the reading light above the lectern. Since he didn't hear HM's request and being fully familiar with HM's peculiar behaviour, he remained blissfully unaware of his failing. HM falteringly outlined the history of M&AD: the people who worked within it and the sort of business profile they specialised in. He was obliged to ad lib much of his planned script as it was difficult for him to see without the overhead light on, and his plight was worsened by the fact that Olin Andersson repeatedly leaned forward, asking him to repeat what he'd just said, as "it was being difficult to hearing over the noise from the fan above him".

HM, with the face of one prepared to kill, concluded his boring speech and exited smartly to the left, while grinding his teeth. Digby stood for his turn and pressed the spotlight switch which he should have done for HM. Angela, the next in line, moved into Digby's vacated chair, and also took the opportunity of reducing the severity of the air conditioner's whining from the control panel nearby. Digby calmly delivered a summary of what M&AD expected their advertising recommendations to achieve, along with the stock blather about the new market opportunities open to BOB, and how M&AD's advertising programme would increase their market share, winding up with a long ramble on his own personal marketing philosophy.

Digby could always be relied upon to overrun his time, and today was no exception to his normal lack of concern for timetables. Each contributor's slot had been accurately timed to the second by HM's stopwatch, and the progress of events was likely to become seriously impeded if Digby did not soon shut up! Digby trundled on, and HM grew more and more restless. He puffed, and sucked in breath, looked at his watch shaking his head. He did anything he could in the hope that Digby would get the message. Digby coolly kept his ground; after all, the BOB people were expressing much interest. Meanwhile, Eve Merrell had quietly moved along into the seat next to Angela and Rod Brody had moved along into what had been Eve's chair. HM's programme was hopelessly shot to pieces

The Besting of Humphrey Mercer

as Digby came to the end of his act, which had been halted several times by some intense questioning from the visitors.

Angela rose and made her way to the lectern, but Digby retreated to the wrong side of the room. He incorrectly returned to the chair he'd previously vacated, which was now occupied by Eve Merrell. HM smacked his hand onto his forehead to the startled amusement of the Swedish visitors, and misinterpreting HM's gesture, a panic stricken Eve hit one of the many buttons on the switch panel. The room was plunged into blackness, and a loud shriek pierced the dark. Angela was instantly bathed in the bright light of a media-planning chart, emanating from the projection room. Columns of journal statistics were emblazoned across her face and spilled onto the screen behind. The AV engineer, confused by the sudden darkness, had switched on a projector. Rod fumbled at the control panel and light was restored. The scream had been the result of Digby inadvertently stepping on Eve's foot before sitting down on her during the sudden darkness. Both were now writhing on the floor. Eve hissed as she massaged a bruised ankle. The visitors from Stockholm were finding it very difficult to suppress their laughter, for they were not certain if this was an intended part of the presentation - a sort of amusing interlude.

'Don't be minding us. Go ahead and enjoy yourselves.' Olin Andersson chuckled, 'We know of your famous British sense of humour,'

'She'll do anything to gain attention,' Digby feebly quipped, as he helped Eve to her feet. She was livid and indignant, as she tried to recover her composure. HM looked as one afflicted by a massive stroke. He sat white and stiff, with teeth set in a frozen corpse-like grin. A ripple of laughter hesitatingly ran around the room. Eve straightened her skirt and limped to her chair, while Angela, seemingly unperturbed, but inwardly unnerved by this embarrassing introduction, launched into her presentation. She heartily voiced her opinions, dramatically building up to the big creative climax, which she and HM had spent so many hours planning and rehearsing.

Outside in the hallway, George Birtles, clad in his cardboard paint tin and ready to play his part in the presentation, was in severe pain due to a distended bladder. It was well past one o'clock, and he had been waiting patiently since noon for HM to open the door with the announcement: "Ladies and gentlemen, I give you Mr. ToppKote!" At this cue, George would burst into the room in his giant paint tin outfit, take a bow and step-out the ToppKote jig to fiddle music, and Angela would read out the ToppKote TV sales message as he danced. To act-out the TV commercial live had been another of Angela's clever wheezes. As the music and commentary came to an end, Angela would then take up a huge paint brush, already charged with red paint, and write her slogan on a huge white board behind her: *Smart guys only do it once with Toppkote.*

That, at least, was how it had been planned at rehearsals.

It was also around noon that two surprise visitors entered the reception of Dynamic House, demanding to see Mr Humphrey Mercer. Ruth Vanderstein politely informed the visitors that Mr Mercer was presently in a meeting, but if they'd like to take a seat she'd get a message to him when he took a break. In the meantime, perhaps they would like some coffee. An agitated but polite Eustace Piggleford glanced at his watch and said that he hoped Mr Mercer wouldn't be too long, and that he and his sister, Miss Peggy Piggleford, would prefer to wait in Mr Mercer's office. Peg sniffed and nodded in agreement. Stephanie was called to accompany the Piggleford's to HM's office, where she left them with an invitation to help themselves to the drinks cabinet.

George Birtles, concluding that the presentation was running seriously late, and in dire need of a visit to the toilet, extricated himself from his cardboard costume, dumped it on the floor and walked to the kitchen.

'Beryl love,' he whispered, 'listen out for me while I go and strain the potatoes. I'll piss mesself if I don't.' He rapidly disappeared. Beryl, misunderstanding George's crude metaphor, and seeing the cardboard ToppKote tin on the floor, assumed that he'd done his dance routine and thought that it must certainly be time for lunch. Beryl determinedly grasped the trolley laden with sandwiches and wine glasses, and proceeded along the corridor towards the presentation room.

As Angela approached the climax of her presentation, HM quietly crossed the room behind her to take his position by the door, in readiness to cue George. A roll of drums thundered from the speakers, HM puffed out his chest and made his dramatic announcement.

'Ladies and gentlemen, I give you Mr. GreatKote!' Angela hissed at him, 'I mean ToppKote!' HM corrected himself, and pulled open the door. As fiddle music filled the room, in walked Beryl pushing the trolley before her wearing a flowery pinafore and a trilby hat rakishly pulled to one side of her wrinkled face, a-la-Greta Garbo. The fiddle music was bluntly cut mid chorus. Having previously learned a few words of Swedish, and determined not to be denied yet another opportunity to expiate her thespian ambitions, Beryl addressed the visitors.

'Gud Moron. Varmast Halsningen to our friends from Stockholm.' Aghast but smiling, the Swedish visitors cheerfully clapped. HM

The Besting of Humphrey Mercer

whinnied, grabbed Beryl's trolley and firmly pushed it back through the door into the hallway, muttering curses and threats to an indignant Beryl. George Birtles re-appeared, hopping along from the other end of the corridor, tucking his shirt into his still un-zipped trousers. HM abandoned the trolley and picked up the cardboard paint tin replica, carelessly lying on the floor.

'You blithering idiot!' he rasped to George, 'get it on.' He rammed the contrivance over George's head the wrong way around and pushed him violently into the presentation room. George could not see where he was going, the eye-holes being at the back of his head, and with his arms pinioned to his side, instead of protruding through the specially designed arm holes, he could neither feel his way around nor re-zip his trousers. He gyrated into the arena, kicking his heels and clumsily attempting to dance in time with the music. Loud laughter filled the room while Olin and his colleagues applauded again. The fiddle music continued and Angela struggled to shout her commentary above the din and laughter.

Olin, who was heartily chuckling, stood and waved his copy of the presentation document in the air and shouted to Angela, 'I think you are not sure how you are spelling Toppkote; my script has it with two "P's"'. HM noticed with gut wrenching anger that George's cardboard replica had TopKote with one 'P' instead of two. Another bloody cock-up, he murmured to himself. Can it get any worse?

Angela was inwardly boiling with rage at this farcical demolition of her presentation. When the music stopped, George ceased his clumsy, blind, dance stepping, and took a bow facing away from the audience with his trousers hanging dangerously below his waistline. HM turned George to face the front while Angela dipped her large paintbrush into a two-litre can of bright red emulsion paint. The door was suddenly, violently, pushed open by someone outside, hitting HM in the back. Rod Brody instantly threw himself against the door, held it closed and locked it. HM bumped into George who slipped due to his disorientation and also because his trousers were falling down. There was a fierce hammering on the door, which distracted Angela as she swung around with the brush now full with thick red paint. The bloated brush caught HM squarely across the face, producing a sharp slap and spattered the room with paint spray.

The violence of the impact caused HM's new spectacles to spring from his nose to the floor where they were trodden on by the gyrating George. Flying paint caused the audience to duck and cover their faces as it flecked the white walls with crimson dots. HM felt the throbbing sting of the impact as he squeezed his eyelids together. Panic overcame him and he was convinced he'd been blinded. He screamed and groped for the door's handle, smearing whatever he touched with red paint. He trod on George who was now rolling on the floor with his trousers around his knees. In an act of heroic desperation, George elbowed and punched his way out of the cardboard straightjacket, eventually emerging with shards of cardboard and paper adorning his shoulders. He stood up in his pink striped boxer shorts and quickly pulled up his trousers while the hammering on the door continued.

HM unlocked the door to allow himself out. It immediately sprung in with fierce energy and smacked him in the face. Eustace Piggleford rushed into the room, threw himself upon Digby and attempted to throttle him. HM staggered to his feet, and the burly Peg whacked him around the back of his head with her large handbag. HM squealed and fled from the scene with his hands wrapped around his red paint-smeared head.

'Where's my wife, you slimy little pervert!' Digby's eyes bulged as Angela and Eve tried their best to prevent Eustace from strangling him. 'What've you done with her; she's left me, you bastard,' Eustace wailed. Tears slid down his cheeks, and he reeked of HM's expensive malt whisky. George Birtles came forward to help, but Peg violently jabbed her heavy knee into his testicular region.

Olin Andersson was no longer amused; he'd seen enough and stood up and thumped the table, shaking with anger.

'Silence, enough of this!' he boomed, and the fracas stopped immediately. 'Are you all mad? Is this a kindergarten? Are you all children?' Olin's imposing frame was trembling and all talk ceased. People shuffled uneasily, as a sobbing Eustace and his sister were hastily escorted to HM's office. Olin sat down, shaking his head. He re-packed his briefcase. 'We came all the way here because we assumed you were all professional and responsible people, but we have clearly been wasting our time, and I do not intend to waste any more!' Those still standing also sat, but Angela remained on her feet and embarked upon a valiant effort at apologising.

By boldly lying, she explained that Eustace was an ex-employee who had been fired by Digby due to incompetence, and that he had clearly decided to take his revenge at this most inappropriate time; she further explained that Eustace's wife was a serial adulterer in whom Digby had no interest. Olin's Andersson's grim face elegantly displayed his lack of faith in this concoction of fiction. He stood to leave.

'Well, I'll say one thing,' he finally remarked, 'this visit to London I shall be remembering for a long time.' The cold and humourless tone of that comment lingered in Angela's mind long after the people from Stockholm had departed from Dynamic House.

Chapter 21   THREE GLASSES FOR FOUR

In HM's office an empty melancholia filled everyone's heart. HM stood dejected and pathetic in his damp, red paint-stained suit. He opened his drinks cabinet and withdrew a bottle of whisky. Everyone had left, apart from himself and the remaining mourners, Angela, Digby and Rod.

'Well, we've well and truly buggered our chances there I'd say,' he bitterly observed, as he set only three glasses on the table. He poured himself a good slug of whisky and slid the bottle towards Digby, very obviously ignoring Angela. His mind was overloaded with mixed emotions and, thinking that Angela was some kind of jinx, did not feel like socialising with her at this moment. Now, to his mind, she had been the cause of Jery's departure, an event he had personally not wished for, she had been directly responsible for the loss of some long-standing business, and now she'd bungled this latest venture.

Angela's eyes narrowed and her face flushed with varying shades of scarlet as she observed the *three* whisky glasses on the table.

'I don't drink whisky!' she pointedly snapped. HM ignored her and looked across to the window. He sunk into a deep and profound gloom, while gazing trance-like at the same setting sun he had so often watched around this time of day, its last flare of gold dazzling, before expiring into a bloody ember, a portent of doom he thought. A B747, like a bright jewel, silently slid across the scarlet fading-to-pewter sky. He wondered if this might be the flight, which was carrying the BOB people back to their own land forever.

'Er, I think there's some gin or vodka in the cupboard,' Digby said to Angela, feeling uncomfortable at HM's unkind cold-shouldering of her. He got up and went to the open cabinet, 'Let's see what we can find you.'

'Thank you, Digby, but please don't bother yourself. I'm leaving,' Angela said, and she looked towards HM. 'You'll regret this, you ill-mannered little shit! I'll teach you to snub me just because you've lost another piece of business through your own incompetence. You couldn't sell a bowl of soup to a starving refugee, you witless little wanker.' HM looked around, he was blood red and boiling with fury.

The Besting of Humphrey Mercer

'I beg your pardon, Miss, you...' his voice failed and his dry mouth rapidly opened and closed in search of the next sentence. Digby and Rod looked away embarrassed, in readiness for the volcanic exchange of verbal abuse between Angela and HM they had so long been expecting. Angela jumped in before HM could recover.

'You should beg my pardon too! It was *me* who had the wit to invent a plausible reason for the appearance of that homicidal maniac Piggleford and his elephantine sister, and if it hadn't been for *me*, he'd have choked Digby to death!'

'Listen, you little bitch, no one told *me* his wife had been coming to town and had been seeing people from this agency.' HM suddenly ranted.

Digby spoke up. 'Now come on, please, let's calm down. It's nobody's fault. We were not to know that Piggleford and his sister would show up. Don't let's start apportioning blame. What's done is done.'

'Well, who let him in in the first place,' Angela returned.

'Yes who!' HM added. 'If it was that bloody receptionist, I'll skin her alive,' he said, dribbling at the mouth after having gulped a mouthful of whisky.

'Now come on, Ruth wouldn't have known what was going on. To her Piggleford was a client, and quite naturally she assumed he had business with you. You can't blame her,' Digby reasoned.

'Would somebody please tell me what that maniac's problem was?' Angela asked with exasperation.

'He's had trouble with his wife; she's gone missing,' Digby explained. 'There was some scandal about her and a chemist bloke, and he thought we were somehow involved, though goodness knows why. Humphrey and I were unknowingly on the same train to London that she and this guy were on, after our visit to Piggleford's factory. He apparently thought I was involved with her also'. HM walked to the window and stared again at the leaden sky. He clasped his glass in both hands and stood, periodically exhaling through his teeth, while occasionally raising himself on his toes to ease the pressure of his corset. He didn't see why Angela deserved any explanation. It was none of her business by his reckoning. She was there to do what she was paid to do and had flunked it. She certainly didn't need to know any more than that. However, he was worried, and a darkness of despair permeated his mind, as he painfully recalled those moments of foolish indiscretion with Angela.

'Thank you, Digby,' Angela said, 'at least you're a gentleman.' She smiled wickedly, and with a contemptuous toss of her head addressed

HM. 'Do you know, Humphrey, you look absolutely pathetic in the photographs? I pity your poor wife.' She slammed the door on leaving.

HM looked around in shocked surprise, taken aback by this unexpected attack. He took another large gulp from his whisky glass, shrugged his shoulders and enquired of no one in particular. 'Huh, what on earth was that all about?'
'You tell me,' Digby followed.

Lionel Butt was not unfamiliar with Angela Bottomly's precocious talents when it came to trashing people's reputations, and he had never been over concerned about his own moral rectitude. But on this occasion he was not fully comfortable with Angela's plan to use his services in connection with the photographs her seedy photographer friend had taken of HM, drunkenly attempting to indulge in sexual acts with Angela and Rosie on the evening of Angela's birthday. It was the suggestion of blatant blackmail he was unhappy with.

Lionel Butt of "Bull, Butt & Bellowes Solicitors" had twice previously assisted Angela in obtaining a handsome settlement for unfair dismissal, as she saw it, from two large advertising agencies she had previously, albeit briefly worked for. At her first employment she had become a junior account executive, her second a trainee copywriter. Both attempts having resulted in failure at both companies for various reasons: bringing drugs onto the premises; a certain lack of creative talent; alleged attempted blackmail; and being caught near naked and in flagrante delicto in the photocopier room at an office Christmas party with a senior director of the company. This little sexual escapade had provided her with a larger pay-off than the amount she had extracted from her first employer, with the able assistance of Lionel Butt, a friend of the family.

But now Lionel was not so easy about Angela's new vendetta against M&AD. Illegally blackmailing HM would not be in anyone's best interests, and with Angela's past reputation, a tribunal's suspicion might be aroused if he attempted to sue for unfair dismissal again so soon, while also asking for a large pay-off similar to the last one. Lionel Butt, whose own grubby interests were more important than those of his clients, set about concocting a better scheme, which would profit them both but with less acrimony and less risk.

Chapter 22   THE LAST WORD

Those now looking for M&AD will not find it anymore. The offices remain, and so do four of the original people, including Ruth Vanderstein, who still sits anxiously behind the receptionist's desk. But visitors will discover a new sign proudly displayed on the door, which carries three simple initial letters.

MBM

'You see, by leaving out one "B" it rhymes with MGM! Sounds all Hollywood, and it's dynamic,' Angela Bottomly, board director, said, as she confidently rationalised to her fellow board directors her idea for the title of the newly formed advertising and marketing company, which had once been known as M&AD. HM was unsure but didn't put up any strong objection, and Angela's most helpful friend Lionel Butt, of Bull, Butt & Bellowes, the agency's new solicitors, nodded his approval. The permanently bewildered Stan Molloy cheered in enthusiastic support of Angela, who had so often kindly helped him up the stairs and into HM's office. She had also on many an occasion adjusted his tie and smoothed down his strips of thin white hair. Stan Molloy thought Angela a "clever and fascinating young thing". She'd pinched his cheek playfully, before taking her own seat at this meeting. HM sat quiet and remarkably subdued throughout the morning's business.

And so it was, on this morning that the four-way partnership of Mercer, Bottomly, Butt and Molloy came into being. A 20% stake in the company had been Angela's final deal with Humphrey Mercer, in return for which Lionel would put some money into the new venture and all photographic and electronic files of HM obscenely disporting himself with Rosey and Angela - among others - would be destroyed.

'This is not blackmail, Humphrey,' she sweetly said to a confused MD, but a new beginning for both of us.' HM silently stared at the sheet of A4 in front of him, slowly nodded and signed. But although all digital files had been deleted, one set of prints however remained in a sealed envelope, in the safe keeping of Bull, Butt & Bellowes. This was Angela's insurance, and the envelope's label was addressed to Mrs Elizabeth Mercer - just as a precaution.

It was a high price to pay for a moment of stupidity, but the deal did include the removal of Rosey to "alternative employment". There was still a problem however, which haunted HM's depressed mind. Despite Angela's sublimely optimistic exhortations that all was going to turn out well, she had developed the habit of publicly making wildly optimistic claims, purporting to be in touch with so many business contacts that she didn't know which way to turn, and the familiar ring of that statement caused HM to lose much sleep. It was true that Angela had introduced a large number of people to the offices of MBM, but no new business had yet resulted, and HM's capital reserves were running low. Between his scant sleeping, he would constantly hear in his mind the queenish summing-up of Angela's half-hour long soliloquy to potential new customers:

"The success of MBM lies in its ability to put its finger on the pulse of market trends, and to produce advertising messages which induce a positive response in customers to the product or service being offered. The result! Increased sales." This sales pitch was usually concluded with MBM's new slogan, penned by Angela herself: *"When the competition stinks is when MBM thinks"*.

It was thought to be rather uncouth in HM's opinion, despite Angela's insistence that only the too old and out-of-date would fail to respond to such a motivating call, and those people who failed to do so were not worth bothering with anyway. He, after all, Angela reminded HM, had screwed-up the BOB opportunity with his ludicrous seating arrangements and military timing plan, coupled with his supposed close acquaintance with Eustace Piggleford. It was largely her cosy, private and personal "evening out" with Eustace Piggleford that had at least secured them his business, for what it might be worth.

Angela's modern attitude was wholeheartedly endorsed by the nodding and beaming Stan Molloy, who had most readily agreed to donate some of his shareholding to her. He thought her a most unusually talented young lady.

Epilogue

'Not too close, not too close, you stupid little bitch!' HM aggressively barked at his driver. He didn't want his car parked close to the kerb lest the door should catch the pavement when it was opened. He immediately held back his anger, shook his head and mumbled an apology. His chauffeur was a sultry woman dressed in a very expensive powder blue, soft leather Chanel suit.

He suddenly regretted his unkindness as Rosey turned to him, pointing a finger to her full, dark burgundy mouth.

'Naughty, naughty boy,' she purred, 'remember what Mrs Bottomly said, you've got to be nice to me!' HM was sitting in the luxurious leather comfort of his new Mercedes, dressed in the finery befitting a successful advertising mogul, but he was unhappy, knowing what lay beneath the smarmy admonishment. 'We don't want 'Liz'beth to see the piccy wiccy's now do we,' Rosey said, with cruel pleasure in her husky voice. HM suddenly sat up straight with a look of horror. Rosey held his shoulders, kissed his cheek and patted his head. 'I'll forgive you, Humpers, but how about buyin' me a nice little pressy wessy. Your wifey doesn't really understand you does she Humpers,' Rosey said, with a mocking simper. Humphrey Mercer thought of Elizabeth and a lump formed in his throat. He loved his wife and it nauseated him to hear his wife's name mentioned by this "handmaiden of the devil", a title George Birtles had conferred upon her when once complaining of her impudence.

Suddenly his hands located Rosey's neck, and he squeezed hard.

'You little opportunist cow,' he screamed as he pressed his thumbs into her windpipe. Rosey's eyes bulged. It sickened him and he looked away. He pressed harder and her long legs kicked and thrashed furiously. She fell into the back seat with HM and her knee caught him sharply in his crotch. He winced but kept the pressure on her throat. She repeatedly jabbed him painfully with her knee, 'Shit, the strength of you,' he cursed. Rosey managed to jab a long-nailed finger into his eye. He screamed and banged her head against the car's window.

A loud knocking at the window close to his ear called HM to his senses, and a stern voice called.

'What are you doing, what's the trouble?' HM felt intense horror coupled with a sick feeling as he recognised the dark blue uniform. His hands immediately relaxed. Rosey was now still and HM gingerly lifted her arm, it was limp, he let it go and it dropped like an unstrung marionette's limb.

Rosey had croaked her last breath.

You may wish to sample other books in humourous vein from Twenty First Century Publishers Ltd.

SINCERE MALE SEEKS LOVE AND SOMEONE TO WASH HIS UNDERPANTS

Colin Fisher is long-divorced with two grown-up children and an ageing mother in care. He is not getting any younger. Perhaps it is time to get married again. There are hordes of mature, nubile, attractive, solvent (hopefully) women out there, and marriage would provide regular sex and companionship, and someone to take care of the tedious domestic details that can make a man late for his golf and tennis matches. All Colin needs to do is smarten up a bit, get out more and select the lucky woman from amongst the numerous postulants. What could be easier?

International best-sellers by Christopher Wood include: A Dove Against Death; Fire Mountain; Taiwan; Make it Happen to Me; Kago; 'Terrible Hard', Says Alice; James Bond, the Spy Who Loved Me; The Further Adventures of Barry Lyndon; James Bond and Moonraker; Dead Centre; John Adam, Samurai.

Christopher Wood has written the screenplays for over a dozen movies, including The Spy Who Loved Me and Moonraker, two of the most successful James Bond films ever made.

'Laugh-out-loud-funny...deeply touching...I _really_ enjoyed this book.' Mark Mills, author of Amagansett.

Sincere male seeks love and someone to wash his underpants
by Christopher Wood
ISBN 1-904433-18-9

www.twentyfirstcenturypublishers.com

CALIFORNIA, HERE I AM

William Lock is in L.A., trying to use his boozy, womanising father's shrinking band of contacts to gain a foothold in the movie business. Not easy at the best of times, but when a rental car disappears into a canyon and Will bumps into an old school chum and loses his heart to beautiful, enigmatic Rashmi, his life will never be the same again.

With Will and his dangerously unpredictable father we survive in Beverly Hills, attempt to hack it in Hollywood, party in salubrious Santa Barbara, hit the slopes in sophisticated Sun Valley and succumb to a date with destiny on a strange Caribbean island where a dark secret from the past and a present mystery await their resolution.

California, here I am by Christopher Wood
ISBN 1-904433-21-9

'A very funny, shrewd and horribly accurate novel about the movie business ... written with sustained brio and mordant intelligence. "California here I am" is also an affecting and moving chronicle of a son's rackety relationship with his father."

William Boyd.

'This is the funniest and shrewdest Hollywood novel I've ever read, and it's a cliffhanger of a story too ... will become one of the great classics of Hollywood fiction.'

Frances Doel, Concorde-New Horizon Corporation.

TOBIN GOES CUCKOO

RUSS TOBIN, the phenomenon created by Stanley Morgan, is back in his nineteenth hilarious escapade.

When the JobCentre suggest they have just the thing for Russ – co-managing CUCKOO COURT, a five-star retirement home – he is sceptical. Why? Because Russ has never managed anything in his life – including himself! Enter the gung-ho American manager Pete O'Shea with a list of tantalising rewards – including the nurses next door – and Russ plunges headlong into a world of genteel chaos.

In Tobin Goes Cuckoo Stanley Morgan gives Russ a run for his hard-earned money – with a parade of weird and wonderful characters hot on his heels.

'Russ Tobin is a genuine original by a first rate story teller.'
Bryan Forbes

Tobin Goes Cuckoo by Stanley Morgan
ISBN: 1-904433-24-3

www.twentyfirstcenturypublishers.com

For something completely different why not take a look at our financial thrillers?

MEANS TO AN END

Enter the world of money laundering, financial manipulation and greed, where a shadowy Middle Eastern organisation takes on a major corporation in the US. As the action shifts through exotic locations, who wins out in the end? Certainly, the author's first hand experience of international finance lends a chilling credibility to the plot. As well as being a compelling work of fiction this book offers, in a style accessible to the layman, a financial insider's insight into the financial and moral crisis, which broke in the early millennium, in the top echelons of corporate America.

Means to an End by Johnny John Heinz
ISBN: 1-84375-008-2

TARNISHED COPPER

Tarnished Copper takes us into the arcane world of commodity trading. Against this murky background, no deal is what it seems, as the characters cheat and deceive. Hiro Yamagazi, from Tokyo, is the biggest trader of them all. But does he run his own destiny, or is he just jumping when Phil Harris pulls the strings? Can Jamie Edwards keep his addictions under control? What will be the outcome of the duel between the hedge fund manager Jason Serck, and brash, high-spending Mack McKee? Geoff Sambrook is ideally placed to take the reader into this world. He's been at the heart of the world's copper trading for over twenty years, and has seen the games - and the traders - come and go. With his ability to draw characters, and his knack of making the reader understand this strange world, he's created an explosive best-selling financial thriller. Read it and learn how this part of the City really works.

Tarnished Copper by Geoffrey Sambrook
ISBN 1-904433-02-2

www.twentyfirstcenturypublishers.com